This collection of eight short stories showcases the multi-genre range of Chad Strong's writing. From Westerns and Suspense, to Fantasy and Supernatural, to Contemporary and Young Adult, each of these stories has been published before, but some are hard to find elsewhere. They are gathered here in one collection in response to the requests of readers. Thank you, and enjoy!

MIXED GRAZING – A COLLECTION of SHORT STORIES by CHAD STRONG
Copyright © 2017 by Chad Strong

First Paperback Edition August 2017

Chad Strong/HunterCat Publishing
Ontario, Canada
www.huntercatpublishing.weebly.com

Publisher's Note: This is a work of fiction. Names, characters, places, and incidents are a product of the author's imagination. Locales and public names are sometimes used for atmospheric purposes. Any resemblance to actual people, living or dead, or to businesses, companies, events, institutions, or locales is completely coincidental.

Book Layout © 2014 BookDesignTemplates.com
Cover Design and Logo by Charlene Raddon of www.silversagebookcovers.com

MIXED GRAZING – A Collection of Short Stories / Chad Strong
ISBN 978-1-988389-00-4

"Blue Sky and Gray Smoke" was originally published online in Frontier Tales, January 2012, Issue # 28

"The Crossing" was originally published online in Frontier Tales, in two parts: April 2013, Issue # 43, and May 2013, Issue # 44

"The Tracker" was originally published online in Frontier Tales, May 2014, Issue # 56

"Deadlock" was originally published in Tyro Magazine, December 1989, and reprinted online in Mysterical-E, Fall 2011

"The Camas Fairy" was originally published in Bards & Sages Quarterly, January 2012, followed by inclusion in Bardic Tales & Sage Advice, Vol V, June 2013

"The Churchyard Incident" was originally published in Death Rattle, a Magazine of Dark Fiction, Fall 2010, followed by Bards & Sages Quarterly, October 2014, followed by inclusion in Bardic Tales & Sage Advice, Vol VII, August 2015

"Stable Hands, Stable Hearts" was originally published in Rawhide 'n Roses – A Western Anthology, March 2014

"The Decision" was originally published in The Hamilton Spectator newspaper, July 2001

CONTENTS

BLUE SKY and GRAY SMOKE

A barbaric yawp surging from his throat, George charged the creek with his rifle, bayonet affixed, clutched tightly in both hands. From the other side of the creek the cloud of gray charged him, itself a screaming, dagger-clawed beast. He was certain it would rake him, tear him. But he was charging forward regardless — the company had their orders.

He heard the captain call out something but he could not discern the words through the chaotic cacophony and commotion about him. Men shouted and screamed. Everywhere, from within their ranks and without, bullets sped from the smoke and the forest like insects on a wild and deadly spree. Mortars boomed and shells soared for the sun. Always, always they fell short and plummeted to earth, whistling their eerie swan songs.

George didn't know which one sang for him, but one of them did. The blast of soil, water, and shrapnel shoved him yards beyond his own stride and slammed him face down on the bank. The ground shook beneath him as another shell exploded nearby. Mud and water sprayed his blue uniform from head to foot. He flung his arms over his head.

The captain's voice came to him through the din somehow, "Who's firing those? Who in blazes is firing —."

George hoped the captain hadn't been cut off as abruptly as his words. He didn't have to release his head and look up to know that the shells were killing both sides. Somebody was making a big mistake.

Something — he didn't pause to consider what — made him look up. A Confederate soldier was coming for him, splashing through the shallow creek with his bayonet ready. With tunnel vision George watched him. Where was his own weapon? His right hand reached around, frantically slapping the mud for the feel of wood and metal. Rocks, mud, reeds. The rebel was only four steps away. Panicking, George twisted and tried to stand.

Searing pain ripped through his left leg and he wailed in shock. Dropping to his knees he spotted his rifle, fell toward it and yanked it upright just as the reb's bayonet slipped through his sack coat and into his left shoulder. The new pain ignited a rage that compelled George to thrust his own bayonet up into the enemy's belly. The blade in his shoulder jerked and in reflex George yanked his to the right. The rebel soldier cried out and fell beside him in the creek.

The graycoat's blade ripped out of George's shoulder as he fell, but George's blade stuck and was nearly yanked out of his hands as he fell forward on top of the other. For a stunned moment George could only lie atop him. Then he saw the red blood oozing from the graycoat's belly and pooling on the surface of the creek water next to him. With a grunt George shoved himself up and off the enemy soldier.

The movement sent pain raging through his shoulder and leg again. He pressed a hand to his bleeding shoulder and looked down at his leg. About halfway below his knee it was gone.

He lifted his face to the smoke-choked sky and screamed. He screamed until there was no breath left in him to scream. He stared down at his severed leg, certain it must be someone else's he was looking at, certain that it was only the grime in his eyes, certain that once he blinked it would be there again. He wiped his eyes with the back of his hand and blinked deliberately. Once, twice, three times. Still the leg was gone. Panicking, he splashed around as far as he could reach, searching for it. It had to be here. But what to look for? Would his foot and ankle be intact or in itty bitty pieces that he would never find scattered all over the creek bank? He'd been wearing red socks, red socks that his mother had knit him and sent at Christmas to cheer him. He was still wearing one.

"I still got one, Ma!" he cried aloud.

The other sock should be easy to spot. He searched up and down the creek with his eyes until his vision blurred and he wavered and slumped into the muck, sobbing. But his sobs ended quickly as he became aware of his lightheadedness. He was losing blood from his wounds. He had better do something about it. Fast.

He removed the bayonet from the reb's forgotten weapon and slit his trouser leg. Tearing off strips of fabric, he bound his wounds as best he could. Exhausted from the effort, George leaned back against the creek bank and closed his eyes. Sleep tugged at him. Sweet, peaceful blackness beckoned. It would be so easy …

A sound startled him — a sound so close beyond his silent sweet blackness that George sat bolt upright. He hadn't even realized how quiet it was before the sound. He looked around. The trees seemed quiescent after the turmoil, their young spring leaves still and silent, half-cloaked in the mist and smoke. Nothing stirred on the battlefield. George saw bodies of men littering the grassy meadow. No one walked among them, checking for fallen comrades they might save. Perhaps he should do that.

George attempted to stand but collapsed back down with a cry of agony. Maybe with a crutch. He could use the rebel's rifle as a crutch. He reached for it. Just as his hand closed over the slippery wet wood stock, a pale hand closed over his. George froze, sucking in his breath. Snatching back his hand he realized the reb was still alive. George yanked his own rifle from the soldier's belly and raised the bayonet to finish him.

But the boy's cry stopped him. Fresh blood brightened his grimy white shirt and soaked darkly into the wool of his gray sack coat. George's eyes scanned his surroundings. None of this soldier's mates were rushing to save him, to kill George for him. Nobody moved. Gray uniforms and blue lay still and silent.

In a sudden flash of panic George cried out, "Johnny! Ted! Burtie!"

He waited. No answer. "Cap'n Tay!" No answer. Not even an attempt at an answer. And still no gray uniforms moved to silence the remaining bluecoat.

George's eyes fell to the soldier he'd stabbed. He was a private, like George. Except for the bayonet he'd stabbed George with, he appeared unarmed. George's arms suddenly cramped beneath the weight of his weapon. He grunted, trying to steady his aim, but the boy moaned softly and George couldn't complete the thrust. He let down the rifle and sighed. For safety he tossed both firearms out of reach of the rebel soldier.

The reb suddenly began thrashing about in the creek, not becoming still until he had flopped, exhausted, onto his stomach. He would drown in moments if George didn't right him.

Fighting the pain in his own wounds George shimmied across the muck and grasped the rebel's coat in both hands. His left arm didn't want to work, but he got enough out of it to haul the boy's shoulders out of the water and lay him on his back on the bank. The reb's cap fell off his head. George retrieved it and laid it next to him.

The boy was blond, a soft mellow blond, except where the mud caked his hair. His eyes opened and closed intermittently and were a bright crystal blue. Fine yellow hairs spread across his lean cheeks like down. His face and hands were fine-boned and he was handsome in an almost pretty way. No doubt he had the girls all over him back home, wherever that was. Unlike George who was short and stocky with coarse dark hair and mud-brown eyes. The girls in Massachusetts had rarely looked at him twice. George guessed the boy was barely eighteen, if that. George himself was twenty-two.

If he let the boy live, he'd have a prisoner. If the reb died, George could walk out of here the only survivor of this battle. Except he might not be able to walk out of here at all. He might need the boy's help.

He cut off the sleeve of his own sack coat and pressed the thick wad against the Confederate's oozing belly. The boy moaned and kicked briefly. George felt suddenly sorry for having stabbed him. But what else could he have done — knelt there and allowed himself to be killed?

He lay back as comfortably as possible and held the pressure on the boy's wound. He stared up at the smoky mist hovering over the meadow and drifted towards peace. In his bliss he woke nestled in deep spring grass and a bright blue sky and his brother's face smiling down at him.

"Come on, Georgie, it's time to go."

"Okay, Peter."

George struggled to sit up and the pain brought him sharply back to the creek. The smell of sweet April grass fled before the acrid stench of smoke and the comforting warmth of that spring sun shrunk from the chill of the murky creek water that saturated him.

He blinked back tears. He had never found his brother. They were supposed to meet in the river meadows at Independence, Missouri, and make that their jump-off point for Oregon. Peter had gone ahead with his wife and two children and George had followed after helping their father clear one more field. George was unprepared for the sheer vastness of the site and the multitudes of people and animals and wagons. He had wandered for three days amongst the crowds and finally lay down one afternoon in a patch of grass, turned his face to the sun and hoped that if he stayed in one spot long enough, Peter would find him. They couldn't go anywhere, anyway, until their guides determined the grass had grown enough to sustain their livestock along the way.

Then the announcement of the war had reverberated through the camp. By the end of the day George had decided to enlist. He would fight for his country and get to Oregon when it was all over. If men like him didn't fight, there might not be an Oregon to go to.

The Confederate boy stirred. George looked over at him and watched the crystal blue eyes flutter open. They darted about with a confused and helpless expression. Then they came to rest on George. They stared at him quite a while before they showed a flicker of comprehension.

"Am I a pris'ner?" he asked with a soft southern drawl.

"Yep. You're my prisoner, seeing as it's just you and me and I got the guns."

The reb's eyes flashed around in astonishment. "Nobody alive but me and a dad-blamed Yankee?"

"That's right," George replied. "Nobody alive but me and a cotton-pickin' reb."

The blue eyes narrowed and glared at George. "If I'm gonna die, I ain't dyin' next to no Yankee!" He slapped George's hand away from the wad of coat sleeve pressed against his belly and struggled to move away, to shove himself up the creek bank on his back.

George bristled. "Well, maybe I'm not so pleased with your company, neither!"

The boy gave up his squirming, his face contorted in pain.

"Besides, it doesn't look like either of us can do much about giving the other some room, does it?" George replaced the wad of sleeve on the boy's wound.

The reb pushed his hand away again and pressed on the cloth himself. "Oh, my gut hurts! Like fire! Whadya have to do it for?"

"What'd you have to stab me for?"

"'Cause yer a Yank — the enemy!"

"Well, you're the enemy, too."

They scrutinized each other's faces in silence. A moment later George asked: "So what's your name?"

The reb looked like he wasn't going to answer at first. Then he said, "Ethan. Ethan Langford Pitt."

"That's some name, Ethan Langford Pitt."

"Well, I like it, so don't y'all be makin' fun of it!"

"I'm not. I just said it was some name. Mine's dull. Just plain old George Dunn. I got a brother named Peter. You got any brothers or sisters?"

Ethan merely grunted.

After another moment of awkward silence George said, "What do you say we get out of this creek and dry off? There's so many of us in it, it's not even running anymore."

"Okay."

With his good leg and arm, George pushed and shoved his way up the bank. Every few inches he stopped to drag Ethan's shoulders up while Ethan pushed with his feet. The blond boy grimaced and bit back cries of pain. At last they were clear of the murky water and lay, exhausted, side by side on the soft green grass.

The smoke was lifting gradually and George's nostrils didn't burn so much from the sulphur hanging in the black powder. The low clouds from last night's rain were breaking up and George could see patches of blue sky way up high above the layers of smoke and mist and cloud.

"D'ya think someone'll find us, George?"

"Sooner or later."

"And they'll take us home?"

"I'm sure of it. With wounds like this, we won't be fighting again any time soon."

Ethan was silent a few moments, then asked tentatively, "D'ya think I'm gonna die, George?"

Startled, George replied, "I dunno."

"I don't wanna die. I promised my ma I wouldn't."

George didn't know what to say to that. "I didn't promise anybody anything," he said finally. "I just joined up and went. I was in Independence, trying to find my brother and go to Oregon. But I couldn't find him. So for a while nobody knew what became of me. I wrote home soon as I could, so my folks would know and they could get word to Peter."

"That's good."

Ethan was silent for a while. George thought he might have heard a bird or two twitter in the nearby trees. That was a good sign, when the birds came back.

"Do y'all believe in God, George?"

"Yeah. Of course I do."

"What do ya think heaven's like? Is it just like they say — all beautiful and perfect and no troubles and no pain?"

"I suppose, since that's what the Bible says."

"It sure'd be nice if it were true. It sure'd be nice if it were true for right here and now on earth, wouldn't it? There wouldn't be this stupid war. I shouldn't oughta be here a-dyin' and neither should you.

"I suppose. My mother always said she's happy things aren't so perfect. Think how dull life would be if everything was always perfect."

Ethan gaped at him with those blue eyes of his big and round like his mouth. "She figgers heaven's dull?"

"She never said that exactly."

"Sho'nuff sounds like it!" The exclamation left Ethan cramped and breathless with pain. When he finally spoke again, his voice was weaker. "I think you oughta pray for your mamma's soul."

"I haven't prayed since my folks made me go to Sunday school, except when it was my turn to say grace at dinner. Once I read about Mr. Thomas Jefferson's point of view, that a man can be a good man without him having to be religious. I cottoned to that right off. Even called it quits with church-going. My folks weren't none too pleased, but I was a man by then, so they couldn't force me. The way I figure it, if I was to start praying now because I'm in trouble, I'd have to be a hypocrite. If God is what the Good Book says He is, I figure He'd rather have me honest than trying to fool everybody just for looks. I sure couldn't fool Him."

"But how'll you be saved if you don't believe? I want you to be saved, George, so we can be friends together in heaven. I'm afraid to go by myself. I'll pray for you, if you want I should."

George felt a lump form in his throat as he watched the earnest moisture make Ethan's blue eyes shine. "Thanks, Ethan. Go ahead, if you want, I don't mind. But no amount of praying will save a man God don't want in heaven, our preacher told us. I'm just a man, and no matter how hard I try, I'm gonna mess up now and then. So I can't ever be good enough. I have to rely on His grace to get me into heaven. So I'll just be the best man I can be and leave the rest up to Him."

"I guess I never thought about it quite that way before."

George noticed the fading energy in his new friend's voice. He remembered what the camp doctor had said about shock. He had to keep Ethan talking, keep him from passing out. He swallowed hard, fighting back a sudden surge of pain from the stump of his leg right up to his spine.

"Well, just think," he began. "If my ma's right, if heaven's perfect, wouldn't you get tired of having everything you want all the time? There wouldn't be anything to wish for. I like wishing."

"God'd keep it in'erestin', wouldn't He?"

"I dunno."

Ethan tried to lift his head to look at his belly. "I don't think I've stopped bleedin' yet, George. And I gotta pass some water."

"Go ahead. I won't look." George turned his face away while Ethan struggled to turn on his side. He could hear him grunt and suck air through his teeth. He knew Ethan was in agony and he hated himself for being the cause of it. His shoulder didn't bother him that much, but his leg throbbed and burned constantly. "I wish I could jump up and run away from the pain," he said as Ethan turned back, finished. "But I suppose that would just make it worse, huh?" He chuckled with self-mockery.

"I wish I could sleep or pass out or somethin'. At least I wouldn't feel nothin'."

"Our doc said not to sleep. Because that's when you go into shock and die."

"I'm startin' to wish I would die. It hurts so bad. And everythin's all turnin' and spinnin'. I'm scared I might throw up."

"I hope you don't. It won't do your gut any good. Maybe just hold your head still and close your eyes."

Ethan tried it.

"Any better?"

"Yeah. Better. It's all black. Nothin' there to spin around. I'm just floatin'."

George brushed a fly from his cheek and raised his eyes to the sky. There was a lot more blue now. Only a few white cotton ball clouds drifted slowly along. The smoke was gone from the meadow, but it hung still as death in the trees.

"That's what it's like after you die," George said softly. "Just like sleeping in pitch black silence. No explosions, no fire flashes, no bad dreams. Nothing. You don't even know you're sleeping until somebody wakes you up. Except it's not your mamma this time. It's God."

"How long 'til He wakes you, George?"

"I dunno."

"Then what?"

"Then heaven, I suppose. Or the eternal fire, depending on what He's got written in the Book about you."

"I think I'm goin' to hell, 'cause I feel like I'm on fire already."

"Naw, you're not goin' to hell. You haven't done anything so terrible. You're just a kid."

"I've kilt people in this war. I tried to kill you."

"I tried to kill you, too. Wherever you're going, I'm going."

"Well," Ethan said with a brave smile, "at least we'll have good comp'ny."

George laughed. "Who wants to go to heaven anyway? Too gosh-darned boring! We'd have nothin' to do but sit around and have our every wish granted every second of every day."

"Yeah," Ethan agreed, sliding like a canoe into the stream of George's vision. "Pretty soon we'd run outa wishes."

"Yeah. Then what? Boring eternity. Forever bored."

"Heaven's so perfect, we'd be perfectly bored!" Ethan howled with laughter even as he clutched his belly in agony.

George crowed in near hysteria. Their laughter died down gradually, like applause for a delightful play. They lay together, chests heaving until their giggles dribbled away.

Drained, George allowed his eyes to close and rested. He slipped in and out of sleep for how long he did not know. He dreamed that the spring grass had grown long and lush about him. He blinked at the ripened seed heads waving in the breeze above him and squinted at the sun hanging high and bright in the clear blue sky. Then his brother's face was smiling down at him and his hand was reaching for him.

"George. C'mon, George, it's time to go."

Smiling, George answered, "Okay. Just let me get Ethan." He reached his arm out and tapped Ethan's outstretched hand. "Come on, Ethan. It's time to go." When he got no response he pulled himself from the dream and tapped Ethan's hand again.

Still Ethan did not respond. George struggled to lift himself up onto his good elbow and look more closely at his friend. Ethan's crystal blue eyes were wide open, staring at him unblinking. His peach-fuzzed jaw was slack, and his lips were parted slightly as if he were about to speak.

"Ethan?" George squeezed the soldier's arm and shook it. The blood-soaked wad of sleeve rolled off his belly and onto the grass. He pressed his hand against the chest. There was no rise and fall of breath. He found the artery in the boy's neck but no blood pulsed there. He waved a hand in front of the pale face. Ethan was already gone. "Aw, Ethan . . . ." George slumped back into the short spring grass. The blue sky above blurred and shimmered as tears filled his eyes and ran down his cheeks to his ears.

It was April now, he was sure of it. He wondered how long it would take for them to be found. He wondered if the grass would grow long and lush around their bodies before anyone came.

With a start he realized that he had never asked Ethan where he came from or what his life was like before the war. Sighing, he figured it didn't really matter anymore where Ethan was from. It only mattered where he had gone. George didn't know how long it would take, but he knew that from this battlefield jump-off point, he would follow Ethan there.

THE CROSSING

Rick Barton grinned the grin of a wolf sated with the blood of a good kill. But as he stood in the doorway of the suddenly silent cabin, his eyes sweeping the sagebrush-studded hills below him, it was not blood that he licked from his yellowed teeth — it was tobacco-saturated spittle. The blood was on his hands.

With one of those hands he took a drag on his cigar and with the other he pulled his woman up against him. Blowing smoke passed her ear he bent his lanky frame and smothered her with a kiss.

"I don't s'pect there'll be anymore cowboys lookin' to play hero after they find *him*," he told her as he straightened up. Still, he had to give the kid his due. The boy had followed him all the way from Spokane Falls, hadn't been fooled by his change in direction after McEntee's Crossing, and had caught up to them in this abandoned miner's cabin just south of Westfield. Barton shook his head, still grinning, and picked up the canvas sacks he'd tossed aside a few moments before. "This fifty thousand is gonna set us up real nice in Canada. I won't gotta work ever again in my whole life. And neither'll you. And I'll let you have all the servants you want."

His eyes stretched into the fanciful distance of his vision, while hers shortened, dropping to the red blotch he'd left on the sleeve of her floral dress.

He shook her, urging a response. "Whadaya think of that, darlin'?"

She looked up at his mud brown eyes, a small smile flickering uncertainly on her lips. Her voice was tight, high and childlike as it found its way out from inside her. "But will they let us go now? You said if we just took the money and didn't

hurt anyone that they'd just forget about it and let us be. But —
." She looked down at the dead man crumpled at their feet. His
blood was still slipping from the knife wound in his chest and
pooling over the hard-packed dirt on both sides of the threshold
of the small pine cabin.

"I told 'em not to follow me!" he snapped. "I told 'em this
is what'd happen to anybody who tried to follow me. It's his
own damn fault." He kicked the body over, out of his path, and
she gasped at the sightless stare of the eyes that seemed
somehow to see far beyond the horizon.

Cursing, Barton took the canteen from her hand, bent and
spilled a little water on the smear of blood on his boot. The
brand new boots had been a gift to his recently deceased Uncle
Alvin from the uncle's best friend. The friend owned a footwear
store in town, and believed Alvin ought to be buried in a decent
pair of boots. Barton believed the low-heeled, shiny black dress
boots were a waste on a corpse, and being the same size as his
uncle, swapped his own worn out work boots for the new ones
the night before the funeral.

"Come on," Barton said, catching the girl's arm. "We gotta
git."

He'd had everything prepared ahead of time — the little
mare stolen for her, the water and grub – everything ready and
waiting for him as he made his getaway westward from Spokane
Falls. It had been a day's ride, and most of that at a hard gallop,
to his late uncle's crumbling old farm house where Barton had
stashed the woman and the mare. During the three months since
his uncle had passed away, Barton had had to remind her almost
constantly to leave off her cleaning and nesting — they weren't
staying.

He led her over to the horses and got her up on the little
cremello mare. Eyeing his back trail as the rising sun stained the
eastern horizon red, he swung up on his spirited bay gelding and
reined north.

Barton set a quick but easy pace for himself, the two horses
and the woman. He estimated another day's ride up to Ragtown
on his own, even with zigzagging through the hills above the

roads, but the girl would make it take longer. No matter. No matter, either, that Barton himself had never ventured this far from the farm on which his uncle had raised him. Spokane Falls had been their lifeline to civilization and commerce. There'd never been any reason to travel anywhere except toward it — certainly not away from it into the wilderness. But with his uncle's passing, Barton had no interest in sustaining the farm. It was far too much work. He'd started hanging around the saloons and the parks in the city, looking for something new.

The old prospector he'd met drinking whiskey on a bench never tired of telling him tales of his twenty years searching for gold up in the Okanagan country. Barton had dismissed him impatiently at first, but then began to listen in earnest as a plan formed in his mind. The old man couldn't read or write, but his recollections were so vivid, his retellings so repetitive, that soon they were as much Barton's memories as the old man's.

And there was no denying the prospector's map had served Barton well so far. The cabin they'd spent last night in was exactly where the old man had said it would be. The fresh water streams had been low, even for this time of year, but they'd been there. There'd been that ranch off the main road where he got food and water and no questions. And now that they were well on their way north, Barton couldn't help snickering to himself.

He'd been very careful to blab around town of his plans to take a wife and move to California, probably someplace cool like San Francisco. He stressed how much he hated the dry plains and longed for the ocean breezes. He'd laid that story on the old man countless times, confident the old coot'd pass it along to anyone who'd listen to him. Nobody'd expect him to take a desert trail up to Canada. Hell, nobody he knew even knew Canada *had* a desert. He sure as hell hadn't.

About mid-afternoon he pulled up in the meager shade of a dry gully overhung with sagebrush more grey than green, desperate-looking shrubs, and shriveled trees. According to the map in his mind, there should be a fresh spring here. He walked his horse slowly around the site and, after nearly mistaking it for a shadow beneath a small ridge of rock, finally found it. It was a lot smaller than the bubbling thing of beauty the old prospector had described, but the water was clean and cool.

Barton lay on his belly, sucking water through his stubbled lips to slake his thirst, and then instructed the girl to get down and get herself a drink before he let the horses at it. Holding the horses, he watched her a moment while she knelt by the still pool, dipping her finely cupped hand into its clear freshness, raising the hand to her lips to sip the water with a dainty femininity that stirred him.

"Best you fill the canteens now, too."

She obeyed without question.

When she was done, he watered the horses and then tethered them to bushes well apart from each other — if he didn't place his gelding out of reach of the mare, she would be constantly nuzzling at him in her apparent need for attention. The bay, while showing no real dislike for the mare, resented her relentless pestering, and had made good on his threats of kicking at her or biting. She'd been discouraged only briefly and always reinvaded his space. The young woman had cried over the patches of missing hair on her mare, so Barton humored her and now tethered the two horses farther apart. Besides, he didn't need a horse going lame from a kick on this trip.

Satisfied that the mare could not reach the gelding, he instructed the girl to bring out the jerky and bread he'd packed this morning. He made himself comfortable in the sandy dirt and began gnawing on the dry, stringy meat. He chewed it a bit, then bit off a hunk of bread and masticated the two together in his mouth, pausing without having swallowed to swill water from his canteen and mix that, too, with the bread and jerky before finally swallowing the whole mess.

After watching him a moment, the girl stooped and brushed the dust from a rock near him, then sat down upon it. She held a small piece of jerky in one hand and an equally small piece of bread in the other. Her canteen she had laid at her feet. Except for a glance back when one of the horses snorted and stamped a hoof, her eyes rarely left Barton. Idly, she took a nibble of her bread.

"Women!" he remarked. "If you could see yerself you wouldn't be none too worried about a little dust on yer rump."

She inspected her dress and the loosened strands of her honey-colored hair. They were coated with a thin layer of trail dust.

Barton laughed. "Don't worry — you can have yerself a bath the first town we hit across the border. Should be Osoyoos — only about five miles over the border, accordin' to my old friend, Mr. Miner." He laughed.

She smiled, grateful, and took a nibble from the jerky in her other hand.

He gulped down his last mouthful and then stretched back in the dirt, pulling his worn hat down to shade his eyes.

"How long are we going to be here, Rick?"

"'Til I says we're goin'," he answered, without opening his eyes.

"What am I going to do till then?"

"Whatever you want. Just don't bug me — I'm goin' to sleep."

She toyed with her meager meal, passing the bread and jerky one at a time from hand to hand. Finally she sighed and began to eat again.

After a two-hour rest to let the worst heat of the day pass over them, Barton packed them up and got moving again. He rode at a walk until dusk, when he found an excellent spot to camp for the night. A tall, long outcropping of rock scattered with scrub curled like a crescent moon around another small but fresh spring. His luck was running high.

He dismounted and, reins in hand, he stretched out in front of the spring and sucked a long drink from its surface, then dunked his whole head beneath. He came up, shaking the excess water from his face and letting out a: "*Whoop!*" His gelding startled backwards, dragging Barton away from the water and forcing him to get to his feet to hang onto him.

"Whoa, horse! Knock it off, ya fool!" he shouted. He jerked hard on the reins. The gelding's head went up and his eyes rolled white, but he halted and stood still.

"That's better." Barton slicked his wet hair out of his eyes with his free hand and stuck his hat back on his head.

He watered the horses before tethering them to some scrub and then picked a comfortable-looking spot to flop over onto his back and stare up at the darkening sky.

"Aren't you going to unsaddle the horses, Rick?" the woman asked, her fingers clasping at the front of her skirt.

"Later. I'm hungry. Fix us somethin' to eat."

"But they've had a long ride —."

He shot up to a sitting position, flinging a handful of sand at her. "I said fix us somethin' to eat — and fix it now!" Then, as quickly as his temper had flared, it cooled. "'Sides, ya gotta let their backs cool some, or they'll swell," he added.

She had flinched, though the sand had not reached her. Now she dropped her eyes and moved soundlessly to fetch the saddlebags. She made a fire to warm the beans and brew the coffee while he dozed. She called to him in a voice he couldn't have heard, then went over and timidly touched his shoulder.

"Supper's ready."

"Good."

He got up and crossed to the fire. It was dark now, and the air was cooling. He ate ravenously while she again ate little. Once sated, he enjoyed a leisurely smoke, then finally got up and unsaddled the horses. He gave them the barest of rubdowns, and then gave them each their measure of feed and made sure they'd be secure for the night. Then he returned to the fire. He sat on a log and stretched his feet out before him. Leaning forward, he brushed the dust from his boots with his bandana, then leaned back again to admire the way the firelight enhanced the sheen and shadows of them. With their flat, comfortable heels, they were boots made for walking, not riding, for being on one's feet all day, not in the saddle, but damn, they were comfortable. Took no time at all to break them in.

He was about to light a new cigar with a twig from the fire when the sounds of people and horses made him drop the glowing twig and draw his gun. The girl hustled up to cling to his left side. Barton dragged her away from the fire and together they peered into the darkness of the northbound trail. The hoof beats and rattle of supplies told Barton their intruders had at least two pack animals. As the newcomers stepped into the outer rim of the fire's glow, a swarthy-skinned man carrying a lantern extended before him called out:

"Helloo?"

"Just freeze right there," Barton commanded as a woman and a young boy came up behind the man, each leading a short, stocky pack mule.

The woman, her bushy hair wrapped in a red and gold scarf, stopped and stared at Barton and his frail companion. She herself appeared as stout as the white mule whose muzzle she slowly stroked. The boy halted behind her, desperately yanking on the halter of his black mule, trying to get it to stop.

The man spread his hands wide. He addressed Barton directly. "We are no harm," he said with an accent Barton could not place. "We are travelers, heading south to join our families before winter."

Barton stepped into the firelight when it was clear the intruders were unarmed. "Well then, keep on travelin'," Barton snapped, waving his Colt toward the trail south.

The man inclined his head almost apologetically. "We have found no place with water to camp for night. You have water here?"

"Plenty."

"Please, you share with us?"

Barton shook his head.

"We have no water for two days now. There is much drought north of here."

"Move on."

"Rick ..." the girl tugged on his sleeve. "They're tired and thirsty. I'm sure they won't take long getting a little water. We could share our fire, too." She smiled at the man's wife.

"Shut up!" He yanked his arm from her grip and waved his gun again. "There's water a few hours south of here. Stay on the trail – you'll find it."

"Not in the dark, they won't – it's too far – the little boy!"

"I said shut up!" He raised his free hand to strike her but before he could the stout woman was between them with alarming speed, the walking stick Barton hadn't noticed blocking his blow.

"Strike her not!" she cried. "Not now – not ever!"

"Not your business!" he hissed down at her through his yellow teeth.

The woman stood her ground and stared back up into his dark and narrowed eyes. "You are on a fool's path," she said. Then she turned gentle eyes on the girl. "What is your name, child?"

"Christiana."

"Christiana — do not let him lead you further. He will destroy himself and you as well. You may come with us, if you wish."

Barton shoved her stick aside. "She ain't goin' nowheres with you! Now git on outa here before I forget my manners and maybe shoot somebody!"

The man called to his wife. "We go."

The woman shook her head at the girl, but stepped back.

"Don't worry," the girl told her, reaching out with her fine hands. "We'll be all right once we cross the border."

"He will make his crossing," the older woman said, holding both the girl's hands firmly in her free one. "But it will not be the destination he seeks. You — you still have a choice."

"I said git!" Barton growled.

The man was passing around the perimeter of the camp, the boy close behind him with both mules. The woman joined them and took her mule's lead rope from her son. They disappeared into the darkness beyond the camp. It was not long before the sounds of their traveling faded from the ears of Barton and the girl.

He glared at her, then holstered his gun and stalked off to urinate in the scrub. When he returned, she was laying out her bedroll. He caught her arm and nuzzled her ear.

"Rick, I'm so tired. I have to sleep."

She had removed her sunbonnet. He eyed her as the firelight flickered in her golden hair and accented the curves and shadows of her figure. "I already made other plans, darlin'." He pulled her up against him and kissed her hard.

She squirmed and finally broke his kiss. "Please, not now, Rick. I'm tired and upset. I just can't."

"Sure you can," he insisted, locking his arms around her like iron bands. "Just give it a minute and you'll want to. You always do." He took her mouth again with his while her struggles only enticed him further.

"Please, Rick — tomorrow."

"No. Now." With one foot he hooked her legs out from under her and fell on top of her on the blankets.

It was well after sunrise when Barton woke. Blinking his sleep-stuck eyes, he reached for his boots. Something rattled in the second one as he went to pull it on. Puzzled, he looked inside and then threw the boot across the camp.

"Jesus!"

A scorpion.

Barton shivered despite himself. It was a moment before he got up and cautiously approached his cast off boot. There was no sign of the crawly thing along the way. He poked at the boot with a stick, flipping it this way and that before venturing to pick it up and shake it out and poke around inside it with a smaller stick. Finally satisfied the threat was gone, he pulled on the boot.

He started a new fire just to calm his nerves before he shook the girl and told her to make coffee. Then he checked his saddlebag to make sure the money was still there.

A sudden impulse made him saddle the bay and ride to the top of the bluff. On the way up his mount shied and skittered sideways on the treacherous rocks. He slapped it with the ends of his reins, not caring what had spooked it. At the top he scouted his route back through the shrub-covered hills as far as he could see. The horse jigged in place, champing at the bit and tossing its head. He slapped it between the ears. "Knock it off, ya stupid —!"

At that moment a dark spot in the south caught his attention. He passed it over, then came back a second time when it appeared to move between two small stands of stunted pines. He strained his eyes to the distance. It *was* moving. The traveler family? No. It was a herd — no — riders.

"Oh, Christ!"

A posse.

He wheeled the horse around and clambered down the bluff. At the bottom he leapt off and ran to the woman still curled in her blankets.

"Get up!" He yanked the blankets off her. "Wake up — we gotta go!"

She stirred, mumbling and blinking. He bent and hauled her to her feet. "Get up!

"Rick ...? What's the matter?"

"The posse's comin', stupid! Now get movin'!"

Her eyes sprung open and he hastily began rolling blankets. She stood motionless, numbed. Then she spied the empty coffee pot near the fire.

"Aren't we going to eat first?"

"No time!"

"But you know I have to eat in the morning. Else I can't function."

He stopped his mad packing and considered it. She might slow him down even more if he didn't let her eat. And his stomach was a touch on the hungry side too. "All right, eat. Just be quick about it. And make me somethin', too. They ain't that close yet." He strode toward his horse and tied on the carelessly wrapped pack.

The further north they rode, the further the shrub-covered hills slipped behind them. Plant life survived only in deep coulees and the trail became more barren. They were completely exposed to the blistering sun at all times now, and had not found water in two days. They were forced to creep over treacherously smooth rock, then to pick their way along jagged inclines, down into gullies and back up the next ridge. He had to stop and pick the reddish brown spines of small, brittle cactus out of the horses' pasterns and fetlocks. Just in time to change direction and avoid it, Barton caught sight of a large rattlesnake loosely coiled on a rock shelf. Beyond the odd lizard scuttling across the ground and a few turkey vultures soaring on low thermals above him, he and the woman were the only things moving in the shimmering heat of midday.

"Aren't we going to rest, Rick?" asked the woman plaintively. "It's so hot."

"This's when they'll rest, stupid," he answered with barely a glance at her. "We gotta stay ahead of 'em."

She was silent for nearly an hour before attempting to speak again. Her voice was little more than a squeaky rasp. Clumsily, almost dropping it, she lifted her canteen from the saddle horn and drank the last of it. Before she recapped it, she patted the lathered neck of her mount. "I wish I could give you some, Creamy. When is there going to be water for the horses, Rick?"

"When we get there."

A jolt lifted her sagging shoulders. "We're almost there?"

"Tonight." He sounded far more certain than he felt.

Her spirit brightened like a newly-lit candle, then abruptly sputtered. "But that's a long time for the horses with no water — ."

"They'll make it."

He watched the thoughts play across her face as she noticed that his mount, too, was lathered where tack rubbed against its body. And all they had done was walk and trot. Had it been two days or three since they'd left the spring? He didn't know anymore. He didn't know where they were anymore according to the old miner's map in his head. He knew there were forested mountains to the west. He knew the great Columbia River was to the east. But he didn't know the mountain routes and he dared not go down to the river road — the law would be looking for him there. He needed to find the old timer's secret route again.

A few hours later he heard her gasp as she woke with a start, having almost fallen from her horse. He glanced back, certain by the look on her face that her heart was pounding with the sudden awareness of her peril. She squinted against the glare, looking for him, and seemed surprised to locate him several horse lengths ahead of her. Her horse had dropped behind and was plodding slowly, stumbling frequently.

"Rick? Rick? We have to stop. I need to rest. So does Creamy."

He looked back at her. He drew rein and his normally spirited gelding halted instantly without protest. Her mount gradually caught up, and stopped when its nose touched the gelding's flank. The gelding did not even flick its tail in protest.

"Please, Rick, can't we stop?"

From beneath the brim of his dust-coated, sweat- and weather-stained hat, he inspected her. Her hair hung in stiff, lifeless coils, plastered to her head with sweat from beneath her bonnet. Her clothes were filthy, her face and hands streaked with dirt. He was aware that he likely looked no better, but appearances were not important right now. His fingers tightened in irritation on the reins.

"Don't you get it? If we stop, they'll catch us! We gotta stay ahead of 'em!"

She made no response, merely stared at him with dull, calf-like eyes. She was so stupid! For the first time, he seriously questioned having brought her along. There would be dozens of new beauties he could have over the border. But he hadn't wanted to wait for them. And if he got tired of them once he did get there, he wanted a woman of his own available.

"Look," he said, speaking as inspiration struck. "Sure, you're tired now, but just think about what's waitin' fer ya in Canada. We'll head for the west coast after you rest up good. It's cool there. Think about our spread, and our big house, and all the land we're gonna have. And all them servants I'll hire fer ya. You'll be a real lady. Think about all them fine dresses I'll buy ya, and all the jewels. We're rich, girl! All we gotta do is get there."

She ran her sleeve across her sticky face, her hand limp.

"But do ya know what'll happen to ya if they catch us?" he asked. "The rest of your life behind bars. They'll figger you were in on it with me — and I won't tell 'em no different if it's yer fault I get caught." He had her attention now. "They'll shove you into an ugly gray prison dress and feed you scraps you wouldn't feed a dog. And you'll have to work. Hard work, girl — every day, all day, out in the crop fields in heat like this.

Scrubbin' laundry'n all that stuff. And no men 'cept the guards and they're mean, I hear. O'course they might not be so mean if'n yer real, real nice to 'em. Know what I mean? And won't one of 'em treat you good like I do."

He saw the horror gradually cover her face as the reality sunk into her consciousness. He grinned to himself. "So you think you can handle a little more heat till it's over, or a lot more forever if you get us caught?"

She nodded, acquiescing.

"Good. Now, listen up. See that bluff over there?" He extended his right arm toward the northwest, pointing until he was sure she had focused on the right one. "You ride straight to it. I'm gonna ride to that one." He swung his arm northeast. "After you get there, head for the one farther on, sorta in the middle. I'll meetcha there. Then we can rest and then it's all downhill to the flats and a few more miles to freedom. Got it?"

"But what if I get lost?"

"Just keep headin' for the bluff and you won't. Look down once you get there and I bet you can see the lake. We can stop on the Canadian shores and drink and swim and wave at the posse. Even if ya think yer lost, I sure won't be, so I'll find ya even if ya do. We gotta throw them lawmen off'n our trail."

"All right," she answered.

Her horse refused to move at first, but Barton slapped it hard with his reins and jolted it out of its heat-induced stupor. He watched her go, and she seemed to be on the right track, so he reined his gelding northeast.

He had to cross back toward her bluff to meet her and lead her down the gullies to the dry creek bed that the prospector had told him never dried up. The old fool must have never seen a drought in all the years he spent up here. Barton's head swiveled nervously at every sound, but he had no choice — they had to ride all the way down to the lakeshore to reach water. He had no idea how long it had been since his horse had stopped sweating, but a pinch of its hide left no doubt that it was seriously dehydrated.

He dismounted and let the gelding drink next to him on the sandy shore. He was careful not to let himself or the horse drink too much at once. Standing, he pulled it away from the water and stared at the girl sitting like a lump in her saddle.

"Get down and take a drink," he told her. "And fill yer canteen." When she did not respond he cocked an eyebrow and a sneer at her. "Did you hear what I said? Get off and get a drink!"

She stiffened in the saddle, and then slumped again, limply dozing in the heat. Her mare's head hung low and still and her nose did not seek the bay gelding.

"Geezuz! You been whinin' 'bout bein' thirsty for hours'n now you sit there like a dumb doll. Well, drink or don't. I don't care!"

He scanned the flats along the long lake and the barren hills of his back trail. So far, no sign of the posse.

He'd for certain strangle that old man if he ever saw him again. He'd assured Barton that there were water holes and creeks aplenty up in those dry hills. They'd almost died of thirst.

He heard the woman getting down behind him. She whimpered and stumbled stiffly toward the water. She'd dropped her reins, but the mare followed her just as stiffly.

"Watch you don't drink too much," he told her. "You get sick on me and I'll leave ya behind." He stood up after filling his canteen and jerked his gelding's muzzle from the lake. The horse was not yet satisfied, but Barton didn't need it succumbing to colic. "Same goes for that mare," he tossed over his shoulder at the girl.

He sat down a few yards from the bank, intending to relax a minute or two. But the gelding kept trying to return to the water. Barton jerked on its mouth repeatedly. The horse was weak, but still determined. "Knock it off!" he yelled at it, tired of this game. Then he noticed the woman sitting in a silent heap on the bank, while the mare still sucked up water as though she'd never get enough.

"Get that horse away from there!" he ordered.

The woman looked up at him, her head wobbling on her neck. Barton grabbed the nearest stone and flung it at the mare. It scored on her rump. She started, but barely lifted her muzzle from the water. Cursing, Barton got up, strode over to her and yanked the reins viciously, hauling the little cremello away from the lake. He kicked the ground near the woman. "Ya stupid —!" Then he spotted the bay heading back to the shore and had to drag the mare after him to catch the gelding.

Holding them both close to the bit, he shouted at the woman again. "All right, enough o' this! Get the hell on — we're movin' now!"

She struggled to her feet, too weary to protest. She tripped over her skirt twice before she made it to the mare. Then she tried to mount, but hadn't the strength. Her hands gripped the saddle horn, and she hung there, exhausted.

Cursing again, Barton stomped over and hefted her into the saddle. Then he snatched up the reins, ignoring the dry lather coating the mare's hair. Mounting the bay, he kicked it and reined north, leading the dehydrated, exhausted mare and oblivious girl.

Still too early for the heat to abate, the sun angled cruelly down upon them. But the dry heat ceased to matter to Barton — he had spotted the distant, shimmering landmarks that the old prospector had told him would put him in Canada.

"We're almost there, darlin'!" he called. He'd expected an elated response from her, but she made none. He turned his head just in time to see her slip from the saddle and fall into a dusty heap on the ground.

"Shit!" He stopped the bay and stepped off. Walking back to her, he said: "Didn't you hear me? I said we're almost there! Ya can see the damn border if ya'd open your stupid eyes!"

He bent and took hold of her upper arms, lifting her to her feet. Her head lolled, and he finally noticed her dull eyes and cracked, bleeding lips. He shook her hard. "Come on, stand up!" But she would put no weight on her feet.

At that moment Barton caught a movement in the corner of his eye. He looked up, and saw six riders a couple miles back. They, no doubt, had seen him as well. "God damn it! Come on!"

He turned her around in his arms and shoved her toward the mare, which had halted right where the woman had fallen. He tried to lift her into the saddle like he had before, but she was lifelessly limp, giving him no help whatsoever. For a brief second he wondered if she was indeed dead, but a tiny whimper escaped her parched throat. Frantically he fumbled with her canteen, pouring water into her raw, parted lips. But she would not swallow.

"Would you drink the goddam water!" He glanced in the direction of the posse. A dust cloud was slowly rising into the still air — they were moving faster now. He grabbed better hold of the woman and lifted. But the instant her weight collided with the mare's side, the mare stumbled sideways and collapsed into the dust with a deep groan.

Standing there with the woman hanging in his arms and the mare flat out on the ground, he screamed in infantile rage. Then he dragged her toward his gelding, tripping over her skirts himself. The bay, as worn out as it was, sidestepped the weight of her as Barton tried to shove her up behind the saddle.

"Why does this have to happen to me?" he screamed to the empty air. A shadow slipped over him, and he looked up to see a turkey buzzard circling in the white sky. Where there was one, there would soon be more. Well, it wouldn't be him they feasted on today!

"Fine!" he yelled into the woman's ear. "You wanna stay here? Then stay!" He thrust her away from him. For the briefest of seconds she stood as though suspended like a marionette, and then she collapsed. He eyed her crumpled form in the dirt, then spun on his heel and swept up his reins.

A shot split the silence, charging the oppressive air with a sudden strange vitality. Barton leapt into the saddle and spurred the horse, whipping it out of its dullness and into the fastest gallop it could muster. He was certain he could make it — the posse wasn't far behind, but the border wasn't that far ahead.

Barton cast a look back over his shoulder and a jolt of adrenalin hit him. How had he let them get so close? No, it hadn't been him — it was the woman. He should've left her a long time ago. Well, she couldn't say he hadn't given her enough chances.

A bullet whizzed by, not three feet from his ear. He yanked out his pistol and twisted in the saddle, popping off a shot at his pursuers. He missed and pulled off two more as he drew within a mile of the border. His fourth bullet found a mark — he saw one of the men almost lose his seat on the run. Barton grinned to himself — he was going to make it.

Then his own body jerked with the impact of the bullet in his right shoulder. It threw him off balance. He overcompensated to the left. His horse, exhausted but still running, stumbled under the strain of balancing this awkward load. Barton pitched forward over the gelding's left shoulder. He twisted in pain, trying to grab the saddle or the horse. His hands scraped the sandy soil. The bay faltered and leapt sideways, away from him. For a split second Barton felt suspended in midair, then his whole body knotted with the impact as his low-heeled boot slipped through the stirrup and jammed his ankle in the twisted stirrup leather. He cried out in pain and anger. He tried to take aim with his pistol, kill the goddamned horse to stop it. He'd run across the border on his own two feet if he had to! Sand and dust invaded his eyes, nose and mouth. He choked. Dropped the gun. He couldn't see the reins he was flailing for. The sand burned through his clothes, seared his skin. Rocks battered him and scrub tore at him.

By the time the posse caught up to the spooked gelding, it had dragged Rick Barton to death over the scorching sands of the Canadian border.

THE TRACKER

Will Sterling rode on at a walk, his palms sweating. He rubbed them, one at a time, against his thighs, resisting the urge to turn his head and look back. He'd seen the quick glance the sheriff had given him. Yet there was nothing unusual about Will. Nothing unusual about his horse. Just an average-looking young cowboy on an average-looking bay cowpony. Did the sheriff recognize him as the youngest son of August Sterling, and did he know yet of the murder? Will didn't think so.

He drew deep, even breaths, wishing his heart would quit hammering in his chest. He rode out the west end of town without being stopped. His stomach grumbled, but even the tempting smells coming from the café weren't worth the risk of questions, or worse, detainment.

The rising sun warmed Will's back and loosened the night's chill from his muscles. The autumn nights were getting downright cold. Last evening, after a half-night and a full day of riding, Will had surrendered to exhaustion and camped in a small meadow he and his older brother Wayne had often used when hunting deer. It had been their furthest camp from home. Now he had crossed into the next county—unknown territory— and he hoped he hadn't made a big mistake.

Once, Will had expressed impatience at camping for the night. Wayne had stood hipshot with his head cocked to one side. "Tracking at night's a fool's game, little brother."

But the night of their father's murder there'd been a full moon and the big round shoe prints from the man's massive black horse had been easy to follow. The killer hadn't even bothered to disguise his trail.

Will knew that Wayne would've been there with him if he could have. But Wayne was off doing his duty to his country, fighting the southern rebels somewhere in Virginia, last they'd heard.

Will wondered if Virginia had forests like here in Oregon, and if they were able to distract Wayne from his thoughts. Will examined the trees flanking the road in detail, but still felt the press of guilt. His mother was alone on the ranch now with his older sister and only a few hired hands. Father was laid out in an empty stall in the barn until the Marshall could be brought. Father was dead—and they all knew who'd done it. Yet nobody seemed to see the need to hurry.

Except for Will.

Maybe they knew who did it but Will had never seen before the tall, thin man who, after riding into the ranch yard and stepping down from his sixteen hand charger as easy as other men stepped off a fourteen-two cowpony, had a brief conversation with Will's father and then shot him in the chest with a Colt .45.

Will hadn't even seen the gun until after he'd heard the shot and he'd been standing fifty feet away and looking right at them. Will's eyes had darted from his father's crumpling form to the gangly, stork-like man. He'd seen him casually holster his gun, turn his back and mount his horse as Will rushed to his father's side. The man rode away at an easy jog-trot while Will watched the life fade from his father's eyes.

Will's ears still rang with Mother's and Abigail's screams. He still saw the ranch hands holding them back and felt the hands dragging him away from the body. Will remembered pointing toward the man rolling away at a lazy lope wondering why somebody didn't shoot him. He nearly climbed over Crinkly Craig Carson who was herding him bodily toward his mother. He remembered shouting and crying but it seemed nobody heard him. Then his ears and his jaws were trapped fast in Crinkly Craig's work-roughened hands and he was staring into the cowboy's eyes.

"There's only three of us here, Will. This is a very dangerous man. We'll send for the Marshall an' make a posse. You look after yer women folk. You the only man they gots now. Ya hear me?"

It took him a second, but Will finally grasped the man's words. He nodded, and when Crinkly Craig eased his grip on him, Will turned toward his mother and went to her.

Mother and Abigail cried themselves to sleep. But Will could no longer cry and he could not sleep. He wrote a quick note, then crept to the pantry and sawed off hunks of bread and ham from their uneaten dinner, wrapped the food in a clean dish towel and stuffed it in his saddlebags. He took the .44 Henry Father had given him for his birthday last year, grabbed a box of cartridges and slipped out onto the porch.

It was three in the morning. All the hands were asleep in the bunkhouse. His path to the barn was clear. Swiftly, he threw every horse an armful of hay to stop their nickering. His chest tight, he looked over the stall door at his father's body, but couldn't go in. He saddled his gelding and led him away from the barn. The murderer's tracks were big round shadows pock marking the earth in the moonlight and headed west. Certain, Will mounted and followed them along the road that led him up and away from the Sterling Valley Ranch.

"How am I supposed to go hunting without you?" Will had asked Wayne when they'd said their good-byes.

"Heck, Squirt, I taught you everything I know about trackin' and shootin'. You're second in the county only to me!" He'd elbowed Will in the ribs hard enough to hurt, but it was a good hurt that Will still carried with him.

All that was a year ago, and now Wayne was gone and Father was dead and Will was fifteen and would have to be a man for his mother and sister, at least until Wayne came back.

His stomach twisted with guilt again. Maybe he shouldn't have left them with just a note. But Mother would've cried and carried on like she had when Wayne had enlisted. He couldn't wait for the Marshall and the posse—it would take them three days to get to where Will was now. If the wind pushing at his back fulfilled its threat of rain, the man and his tracks would be long gone.

It was daylight now, and those distinctive tracks were easy to follow, even mixed in with others from the town he'd just passed through. Will figured the massive black horse might've been a draft cross, even without the telltale heavy hair around its pasterns. If it was a purebred, it was a breed he didn't recognize.

The road crested a hill and ran down into a heavily forested valley, cutting through the trees as straight as a line down a dun's back before disappearing around a ridge. Will halted at the top of the crest and surveyed the view. Not a soul on the road besides himself, and forested hills as far as he could see, broken now and then by rocky outcroppings. A gap in the trees showed him the glint of a river running along southwest of him.

He clucked his horse forward and set him to an easy lope. He needed to cover some miles and catch up to his prey. Healthy caution made him slow up as he approached the sharp curve he'd seen from the rise. He rounded the corner wondering if he should've loaded the Henry. Wayne had always refused to allow him to carry the weapon loaded—it could be set off accidentally far too easily for Wayne's liking. There was no sign of danger as Will walked on around the bend. He squeezed Sonny back into a lope and was a half-mile down the road when he realized the tracks were gone.

He drew rein and scanned the ground, carefully serpentining back the way he'd come, his heart pounding in his chest and a feeling of foolishness rising in his throat. It had been really easy to this point. Maybe too easy.

At last he found the place where the man had left the road, taking a path overgrown and crowded with trees. Stupid, stupid, Will scolded himself. I rode right by it. Shoving his hat down tighter on his head, he ventured onto the path.

Time to slow down. Time to think like a hunter. It should be easier than finding deer. A horse that size would be hard to maneuver in the bush. Hard to hide. Hard to keep quiet.

A light breeze fluttered dry golden leaves clinging to white-barked poplars while spruce and pine stood still, dark and silent. The underbrush was a mix of golds, browns, and reds, and Will heard the occasional scurry of small critters amongst the fallen leaves. Above him a few sparrows twittered and somewhere an eagle cried.

Stopping in a small meadow, he got down to loosen Sonny's cinch and let him graze the fall grass. Will dug into his saddlebags and chewed off hunks of bread and ham and washed it all down with water from his canteen. He was careful to eat just enough. He didn't know how long he'd be out here.

He gave his horse thirty minutes to graze. He was itching to go once his hunger was sated, but occupied himself with watching the shadows of clouds pass across the ground. The white bark of the poplars turned grey in the cloud shadow, then blazed brilliantly white again as the sun came out. The trunks of the older trees were blotched with black and deeply fissured. The quivering leaves flashed like gold pieces on the branch tips.

If this man was as dangerous as Crinkly Craig had said, there might be a bounty on his head. They'd need it now that Father was gone. For certain Will would bring that magnificent black horse home to keep.

"That would be somethin', wouldn't it Sonny?" he said to his mount as he tightened the cinch. "Not that he'd ever replace you." He ruffled Sonny's black mane and stroked his reddish brown neck. "Well, we gotta get goin', buddy."

Will stuck his boot in the stirrup, swung up on Sonny and started down the trail. Snapped branches and trampled underbrush made the large horse's passing impossible to miss. Will's cowpony had an easier time of it, following the wake of destruction.

The trail descended toward the river valley Will had seen from the rise. He could see the shadow of the crease between the mountain ridges, but not the river itself. The trail became dangerously steep. The black horse's hooves had slipped and scarred the earth on its way down. Will nudged his horse on cautiously, feeling the bay's hooves slide beneath him, tearing up moss and raking across exposed rock. He brought him up on a sizable ledge to let him rest while Will looked around and got his bearings.

The rocky ledge jutted nearly forty feet out beyond the mountain trail and swept steeply down into the valley. Here Will appreciated a nearly unlimited vista—everything except directly back the way he'd come was a grand open view. Orange sunlight sparkled in the mist rising from the turbulent falls spilling out of the hills. From the base of the falls the river meandered along an irregular path, pressing beneath eroded banks, withdrawing from dry exposed stones, shimmering over rippling shoals, and swirling in deep clear pools.

A stray rain drop against his cheek reminded Will that the autumn rains were coming. By spring the melting snow would add to the runoff and the river would become a raging torrent, far different from the placid wanderer it now appeared. Along its approach toward Will, the river slowed, winding down into the marshy bottom land and appearing as still as death in a large bog two hundred feet below Will. Movement caught Will's eye and his heart jumped as he saw his father's killer trying to negotiate the edge of the bog. It appeared the man had thought he could skirt around it but, except at his entry point, the cliff edges were too steep. Will would never have attempted that. The bogs were too dangerous, unpredictable in depth, and completely concealing of horse-maiming hazards like old deadfalls and sharp rocks.

No sooner had the thought run through Will's mind than the big black horse began to flounder. Rearing and pitching, it tried to escape the sucking wet muck. Abruptly the man leapt off and sank to his knees in the quagmire.

Springing off Sonny, Will yanked his rifle from the scabbard, dropped to one knee, and started stuffing cartridges into the long tubular magazine. Shouldering the weapon, he took aim and fired. At that very second the flailing black horse threw itself sideways toward the man and Will's bullet punctured its throat. The horse squealed in pain and flung itself madly about before collapsing into the bog.

"Oh my God." Will said aloud as he rose to his feet, stunned at his error. The horse . . . the magnificent horse. "I'm sorry," he breathed, though neither man nor horse would have heard him.

Tossing Will a glance, the man struggled to examine his downed mount in the mire. He brushed the back of his hand across one cheek. Before Will could shout "No!" the man pulled out a revolver from beneath his long black drover coat and shot the horse through the forehead. Reaching low over the saddle, he then withdrew a long gun, raised it, and fired a shot towards Will.

Will gasped, too late realizing he was skylined to the killer. Sonny grunted behind him and collapsed onto the rocky ledge.

"No!" Will screamed and threw himself down next to his horse. "Sonny!" The bullet had penetrated the heart. The kind of perfect shot Wayne would have insisted upon while hunting deer. Sonny's breathing was labored for a few moments, and then the horse was still.

Tears spilled down Will's cheeks, leaving clean tracks in the grime on his unwashed face. He sobbed loudly, without shame, wetting Sonny's face with his tears. Choking, he sprang to his feet, snatched up the Henry and shook it over the edge at the man below. "I'll kill you! I'm going to kill you!" His words carried well in the clear morning air.

"An eye for an eye, laddie! We be done now! Let it be!" the man called back, and sent him a single wave of his arm as he stepped, stork-like, away from his horse and disappeared behind a bluff of rock and bush.

Will screamed with guttural, primal rage, shouldered the Henry and fired shot after shot at the man's last known position. He fired until the rifle was empty and his hands burned with the pain of trying to hold onto the hot steel barrel. He screamed until his lungs were spent, and finally collapsed onto his knees on the rocks. His chin on his chest, his shoulders heaved, and then he retched his breakfast onto the ground before him.

How could things have gone so wrong? It wasn't supposed to happen this way!

He had no idea how long he'd knelt there when a stiff breeze pushed at him and a pine cone fluttered past him on the ground. The wind renewed its warning of a storm. Will didn't care. He'd just as soon sit right where he was until he died. He wished he were dead instead of Father and Sonny. They didn't deserve it. He did. He'd killed that beautiful black horse that was no more guilty of anything than Sonny. Will had messed up—it was his fault Sonny was dead.

The wind shoved at him in earnest now. Large raindrops tapped on his hat. He had to get off this exposed ledge and seek shelter. He turned to Sonny. There was no way he could move the horse. As the clouds darkened above him, he gently removed

Sonny's bridle and undid the cinch. It took a lot of tugging to free the saddle, but eventually Will got everything off the horse. With one last good-bye, he hoisted his gear and lugged it into the forest as the rain began to strike him more fiercely.

A forest was not always the best place to be in a windstorm, but bald exposure was worse than the threat of a tree coming down on him, Will figured. He found a rock ridge covered with moss and draped with ferns that would save him from the worst of the wind. It was flanked by several fir and hemlocks that would keep out much of the rain. There was little sense in looking further. He shrugged into his slicker and then stowed his gear beneath the fir that seemed most dense. Crawling in after them, he made himself as comfortable as possible and pulled the Henry up close.

He was afraid to make a fire in this furious wind, even if it would light in the rain. As he peered out from the green canopy of the tree, every waving branch startled him, every snap of a dead limb rattled his nerves. His eyes strained to decipher movement from movement, shadow from shadow, and he suddenly noticed how much harder it was getting to see. It was now mid-afternoon, but it seemed more like twilight in the deepening darkness.

If his father's killer chose to come back for him, Will feared he would neither see nor hear him coming. It was next to impossible to separate the motion of a live body from all the motion of the trees and shrubs in the wind.

Would the stork-like man come back? Will realized that in all the time he'd spent balling on the ledge, the killer could have crept back and finished him. Why hadn't he? He'd said something about being square now—an eye for an eye. *A horse for a horse*. More tears slipped down Will's cheeks. He hugged himself against the cold and rocked back and forth in the gathering darkness.

He woke with his slicker choking him, lifting his shoulders from the ground. He didn't remember falling asleep. Will clawed at his slicker, trying to drag himself out of the black pit of exhaustion he'd collapsed into. His hands closed around gauntleted leather gloves. Gasping, he came fully awake and stared into the face of his attacker. The face was merely a shadow in the darkness. Water dripped from the brim of the man's hat onto Will's face and the smell of whiskey and oilskin wrinkled Will's nose. He struggled, but the harder he fought, the tighter the grip at his throat choked him. The hands shook him.

"Be still, lad! And listen well. I'll tell ye this only once."

Will quit struggling, and breathed through his teeth.

"Your heart's hurtin', I understand. But ye understand this—your father and I, we had business between us. And a bad business it was. Your father wronged me and mine in a way he should not have. And he knew the outcome of that wrong, but his greed and his pride pushed him beyond all reason. I delivered the retribution he believed himself beyond."

"What —?" Will began, but a quick, hard shake of those hands silenced him.

"My father took his own life after yours took his land. Land he did not need—only wanted."

"My father wouldn't —!"

"Be silent! Listen and make not the same mistake your father did. In your pain, ye've taken my horse. In turn, I've taken yours. Now let it be. Proceed further than this and it's only your pride. This chase ends here and now. Or it's your life that does. Understand?"

Will did not understand. The grip on his throat was so tight he couldn't speak. He managed a grunt and the barest of nods. The man seemed satisfied. He released Will.

"Ye're a brave lad—use yer bravery where it best serves. Now go home to your women. Be the man they need ye to be. Be a better man than your father."

The man turned and his oilskin coat scraped the low tree branches, knocking a spray of rainwater onto Will's prostrate form. Will tried to get to his knees but his stiff, cold muscles refused to obey him. By the time Will had gotten out from under the tree, the man had vanished into the wind-lashed forest.

What did the stork-like man mean? Will's father had cheated the man's father out of his land? Will couldn't fathom it. August Sterling was well-respected in their county and others. Many people sought him out for his advice and opinion on all sorts of matters. Will couldn't imagine him cheating anyone. The ranch was prosperous—there was no need.

The stork-like man must have been misguided. There must have been some sort of misunderstanding. And just my pride that keeps me chasing you? No! You killed my father, you bastard. I'm going to kill you, and that's justice, not pride!

Will sat huddled within his shelter, shivering, sleeping only in snatched moments when his exhausted body and sorrowing heart let his consciousness slip away.

Morning dawned damp and cool. Low clouds breezed across the sky, concealing and then revealing the sun in irregular, unpredictable bursts. Will ate some of his cold ham and bread and drank from the canteen. Packing his saddlebags with only essentials, he slung them over his shoulder. Picking up his rifle he stepped into the tracks of the black-clad killer.

It was uncanny how the stork-like man had followed Will's trail from the ledge through the pitch black forest to his crude, cramped shelter. But as he walked back out, Will realized his own path had been wide as he dragged his saddle and other gear the clearest possible way through the trees and underbrush. He had taken no care to avoid damaging the plant life, or his saddle for that matter, in his haste to find shelter.

As Will reached the ledge he tried to resist but his eyes pulled him to the lifeless body of his horse. Several ravens were hopping about Sonny's body, pecking at it.

Exploding with rage, Will dropped his burdens and ran toward them, arms and legs flailing. "Get away from him! Get away!"

The ravens took flight and settled in the high branches of nearby trees. They cawed at him. They would wait until he was gone, and then they would return. Will stood stiffly, panting, his heart pounding, his head swimming.

One raven, bolder than its fellows, launched from its perch and arced down toward its interrupted meal. A shadow slipped over Will's head and the largest bald eagle he'd ever seen struck the raven bodily, sending it tumbling into the abyss beyond the ledge. The other ravens squawked and scattered as the eagle swept upward into the sky.

Will recalled Wayne telling him once that an eagle could strike its prey with twice the impact of a rifle bullet. Though he raised his arm to shade his eyes, Will lost sight of the eagle as it flew across the sun. Maybe it had made a dive to catch the raven. Maybe it would return to claim Sonny as its own.

With the ravens gone, the ledge was still and silent. Will didn't want to look, but he saw the damage they'd already done to Sonny. He knew he couldn't leave without allowing them, or the eagle, to do as their natures demanded. Resigned, he turned and went back to his gear. Kneeling, he picked it up. Refusing to allow himself one last look, he started down the rocky slope to the edge of the bog.

The stork-like man had retraced his steps to this point. He would have passed his horse in the dark. Will did not look too closely at the great black charger. He concentrated on discovering where the man had gone from here.

Thick groves of ash trees surrounded the bog, through which Will could see no clear passage of the man. The tracks through the bog itself were a chaotic mess. Continuing on the assumption that the killer was back-tracking himself, Will slogged through the quagmire looking for his exit point. He found where he had likely gone, only to lose the trail in the climb to higher ground. Frustrated, he fought his way back to the bottom of the ledge trail and stood there, soaking wet and breathing hard.

His heart nearly stopped when he suddenly realized that he was standing there, a still, perfect target. His head twisted around at the sound of a bird fluttering through the bushes. His eyes scanned the hillside. The man had warned him not to follow. Was he hiding in the trees up there, just waiting to take his shot?

As he moved for cover his eyes caught something different. A line of bushes led his eye along a narrow horizontal ridge at the base of the mountain, about forty feet above the bog where the ash grove began to transition into a mixed forest of pine and other species. From this angle, the leaves along that sight line appeared slightly lighter in color than the surrounding foliage. Will inspected them closely and found them to be dry. Yet on either side of the line they created, the bushes were still dripping wet. He studied the ground, and at last found a boot print in the rocky soil beneath them. Reinvigorated, Will followed the trail as it skirted the bog. This trail was fresh—the rain had ended shortly before dawn. The killer had obviously passed through afterwards.

The trail led him up the far side of the mountain, where Will stopped to rest and take his bearings. It was beautiful country. Below him ran a narrow gorge, at the bottom of which trickled a small, clear creek. Something moved. Will expected a deer, but the shape rose from the water tall, thin and stork-like—his father's killer!

Instantly, Will dropped to the ground. He laid absolutely still, his heart hammering in his chest. He couldn't hear anything over the blood pounding in his ears. His faced pressed into damp green moss, he dared not move. Several minutes passed before his body calmed enough that he noticed the scent of the earth and the sound of small animals around him. Only now could he trust himself to draw his rifle to his shoulder. He would not make the same mistake this time. He would be sure of his target, and make one single kill shot.

Slowly, soundlessly, he raised his head from the ground just enough to see over the lip of the ridge. The stork-like man was still there. He was sitting on a large boulder, his back angled to Will's position, and appeared to be eating something. Will estimated the distance at just over 150 yards. The breeze was almost non-existent. He could make the shot. Easily.

Tucking the butt of the Henry tightly into his shoulder, he propped his elbows firmly and comfortably into the earth, and sighted his target. He began to breathe slowly and deeply, as Wayne had taught him, becoming one with his weapon, his environment, his prey, himself. He visualized the bullet punching through the ribs, tearing through heart and lungs. Soon the ravens would be picking at the stork-like man's dead flesh.

The stork-like man. A man. Not a deer. Not a source of food. Just a long-limbed lump of flesh and blood left to rot in the woods.

He deserved it. He needed to be put down like the killer he was.

Mother and Abigail would sleep in peace. Wayne would be proud of him for delivering justice to the man who had murdered their father. Father would appreciate the retribution. Father had used that word a lot. He had ranted often of his view of fairness and having the might and right to meet it out.

Wayne would approve of Will's having tracked the man relentlessly. Of not having given up. Of the way he now had his shot set up.

But of shooting a man in the back?

Will nearly called out to the killer, to make him turn around.

The cold dampness was seeping from the earth through Will's clothes, chilling him. With the mountain behind him the autumn sun would never penetrate to his position on the ridge. He would suffer from exposure if he didn't move and warm his body soon. He had to take the shot, make his kill, and get moving home.

Fairness. What was fair and right about killing a man without looking him in the face and both of you knowing why? The stork-like man had given that much to Will's father. As Will watched, the man turned his left cheek into profile for Will, lifted his face, and scratched at the dark stubble under his chin. Again Will nearly called out. But he did not, and instead lay in the cold wetness observing the man as he imagined a god would. He felt like the eagle that had struck the raven, with the power of delivering unforeseen death at any instant.

The stork-like man rose from his boulder, bent, and snatched up his pack from the ground much like a stork would snatch a fish or a frog. He shouldered it and, one at a time, stepped his long legs over a deadfall and began to walk along the creek, away from Will.

Nearly panicking, Will shifted his rifle to follow him. In less than fifty yards the man would be out of range. The open forest allowed Will a number of opportunities for a clear shot. Will took none of them.

"We be done now," he said quietly, just before the stork-like man vanished around a bend in the gorge.

DEADLOCK

"Where the devil is he going?" cursed Tom Mallory as he shifted into low gear. The bumps and potholes in the dirt road allowed his car nothing more than an arrested crawl. The dark night made it even more difficult to drive in unfamiliar country. At least his quarry was no better off. *If he thinks I'll get tired of chasing him*, he thought, *He's not half as smart as he thinks he is.*

But McKenzie was smart — that was the whole problem. He was still loose after having murdered at least seven people — two of whom had been cops. And of those two, the last one had been Mallory's half-brother, Ted. He and Ted were ten years apart, but Ted had been a nice kid. Too nice to have to endure what that bastard had put him through. Too nice to be dead at twenty-three.

Ted had looked up to Tom ever since Tom's widowed dad had married the kid's deserted mother. The kid had had a hard time early in life. Things had turned around for him. He became a cop because Tom had been one, and was working his way up to detective just like Tom had. Only the kid didn't make it.

It was just dumb luck that he'd walked in on what was called in as a domestic violence. He wasn't prepared. Tom knew he would never forget coming on to the scene hours later. Nobody'd told him. He walked into the back bedroom. There were three bodies in there, each of them in more pieces than Tom would have thought possible. One of them was Ted's.

He shivered so violently the steering wheel twisted and the car bounced off a rock on the side of the road. "Jesus, Mallory, watch it!"

He regained control of the car. It wasn't even really his car — McKenzie had shot the tires out of his Dodge on a back road just outside of Stoney Creek. Mallory had radioed his position, then hiked three kilometers into town and commandeered the Toyota from a couple of high school kids hanging around outside the local convenience store. They'd stared at him and his badge with awe, like they were watching some TV cop movie.

Thanks to reported sightings of the old Chevy McKenzie had stolen, Mallory had finally picked up the man's trail again. Some thirty-odd kilometers later, he caught up to him somewhere in the hilly farm country outside Caledonia. The dirt road McKenzie had chosen to try to lose him on twisted through the darkness like a slithering serpent. As Mallory tried to speed up the taillights of McKenzie's vehicle vanished. Mallory drove as fast as he dared, trying to catch up again. The road smoothed out and he picked up speed. His headlights showed him no curve in the road, no hill of any sort. McKenzie hadn't been that far ahead.

He shoved the brake pedal to the floor and searched the blackness. The lights had disappeared right about here. Had McKenzie shut them off? Had he turned off somewhere? Mallory saw nothing, heard nothing through the open window but the breeze rattling crispy leaves.

"Damn!"

He shifted back into gear, rolling slowly, the tires making more noise on the fallen leaves than the rumbling of the engine.

Wait! he thought. *What if that's what McKenzie wants you to do? What if his car's hidden in the trees, and what if he's waiting right now for you to roll right by him so he can grab you and kill you like every other cop who got too close? Like Ted?* His foot pressed the accelerator all by itself. The car fishtailed, spewing dirt and leaves out behind him. Ted's decapitated head swam before his eyes. Mallory's hands covered his eyes. He fell against the steering wheel. It was then that he realized he'd stopped the car.

"Get a grip on yourself, Mallory," he said aloud.

He wasn't going to do Ted or any of the others any good if he lost his head. With a bitter snort, he knew that that would be exactly what would happen to him if he didn't pull himself together.

He reached for the stick, pressing his palm against the smooth round knob. As he was about to put her into first he noticed a driveway on his left. There was no moon, but the starlight let him see the outline of a building, like a black void, at the crest of a low rise.

Had McKenzie pulled in here? Or was Mallory sitting here like an idiot staring at a sleepy farmhouse while that monster was getting further and further away? He nearly drove on, but his gut said here. It was all that made sense. He backed the car up enough to turn in, and drove up the driveway.

Near the house there were two vehicles parked beneath an immense maple. Mallory shut off the engine, listened, and looked. He got out and gently closed the door. Then he wryly wondered why. In this lonely country, if McKenzie were here, he would have already heard the car pull up. Mallory walked toward the two cars. The one furthest from the tree was a dark color. McKenzie was driving a brown two-door Chevy. He drew his Smith & Wesson short Magnum from beneath his jacket and checked both cars. Empty. The two-door had no plates — part of McKenzie's M.O. Mallory laid his hand on the hood. It was warm. McKenzie was here.

The place looked quiet. Maybe no one was home. It was a Friday night, somewhere around 3 am, but that didn't mean much. He hoped to God there was no one in that house but McKenzie.

He made a quick call on his department issued cell phone to report his approximate position, although he knew he couldn't count on back up any time soon. Crossing the lawn, he went up the porch steps to the front door. The screen door inevitably squeaked. He tried the knob on the storm door. It wasn't locked. He balanced the screen on the fingertips of his left hand and, with his .357 in the right, pushed the wooden door open quietly. He checked the hall, all was clear. Sliding in around the frame he let the screen door squeak closed behind him.

He fished his Sure-Fire flashlight out of his jacket pocket and used the push button on the end to send brief shots of light where he needed it. There was a bedroom on his immediate left, a wide entrance to the living room a little further down on the right. The floors were hardwood. The hallway had a carpet runner down the middle. He stepped to the doorway of the bedroom and let his gun precede him in. The room was empty. The bed covers were mussed. He prayed these people were slobs rather than victims. The floor creaked under his foot as he leaned over to feel the center of the bed. It wasn't very warm. Could be there hadn't been anyone sleeping in it.

He left the room and proceeded down the hall. Next on his left was a bathroom, also empty. At the end of the hall there appeared to be another bedroom. It was even darker at that end of the house. His toe kicked something small. It made little noise but he froze anyway, listening for McKenzie to rush him. Nothing. He felt for a light switch, found it, and flicked it. No light. That's what he figured. He drew a breath and stepped in.

As his eyes adjusted, he focused on some sort of mobile hanging from the ceiling over the small bed. The covers of this one were mussed as well. Shapes, shadows, were stuffed toys. This was a child's room.

His body jerked when he heard, felt, the dull thud from the living room. First satisfying himself that no one was concealed in the bedroom, he left it. He edged his way back down the short hall, acutely conscious of his rapidly beating heart. He hoped McKenzie stuck true to his M.O. He'd never harmed a child. But there'd never been one present in any case Mallory knew of. When he reached the entrance into the living room he crouched low, pulling deep, even breaths into his lungs. With an effort of will he steadied himself, relaxed, lowered his heart rate. He listened, silence piercing his ears.

He saw that the couch split the living room in half, its back to the kitchen doorway, while it faced the front windows. A couple more chairs, tables, lamps, the usual furniture. The couch was closer than the open doorway. He gathered himself to move quietly but quickly. Three bent strides gained him the arm of the couch and a forth one got him safely behind it. He squatted and peered toward the kitchen.

It was all so quiet — perhaps McKenzie had escaped out the back. At once, a crash spun him round and he brought his gun to bear on — a little girl.

She screamed. Three bullets tore into the chair and the couch as Mallory grabbed her arm and hauled her behind him. He pinned her down as he crooked his arm around the couch and sent a few rounds back at McKenzie. The child shrieked, wailed, and kicked. Mallory smothered her mouth with his hand.

"Shh! I'm a police officer. I'm here to help you."

She must have understood him for she was suddenly still. She sniffled and choked, but she was trying to stop crying. Mallory was trying to hear whatever McKenzie might be doing. Anything was difficult to pinpoint over the child.

"That's a good girl," he whispered to her. "My name's Tom. What's yours?"

"S-Samantha."

"Where's your mommy and daddy, Samantha?"

"Daddy's away. He's got Mommy."

He? "Who? Your daddy?"

"No. The - the man..."

Oh, dear God. "Do you know where she is?"

"Down in the basement. He tied her up. I saw. I'm hiding."

"Good girl." With his free left hand, he brushed aside pieces of the ornament she'd broken.

"I've got the kid's mother!" McKenzie yelled suddenly. "I ain't started on her yet, but I will. D'ya wanna watch? I heard you saw the last two! Is it true one of 'em was your brother? Didja like how I left 'em? Didja like it, cop? D'ya wanna look just like 'em? I do beautiful work, ya know!"

McKenzie stopped talking as his cackling chuckle rose in his throat. Then he went on: "I couldn't never decide if I wanted to be a doctor or an artist — don'tcha think this is a good compromise?" He roared, this time a big booming laugh. "Why don't you answer me — Mallory, ain't it? Why don't you answer me, Mallory?"

"I'm too busy picturing you carved up!"

McKenzie howled.

Before he'd even finished saying it, Mallory half-regretted it. It was what he wanted right now, but he was letting his feelings froth too thickly, too high. "I don't suppose you'd give yourself up quietly?"

"Not on your life!"

"I'll make you a deal. You take off right now — leave the lady and the kid with me."

"Uh-uh."

"Why not?"

"'Cause that's what you want me to do." McKenzie paused. Mallory heard him scratching himself in the darkness. "Besides — I ain't had my fun yet. I always finish what I start. The lady's down there waitin' for me."

Mallory responded directly, "You're not gonna start her, McKenzie. You're not gonna touch her."

"Oh?" said McKenzie with a touch of irritation and doubt in his voice. "And what are you gonna do about it, cop?"

Mallory saw a thick tree-branch of an arm point level across the doorway.

"The basement door's right here. All I gotta do is open it and walk down."

"You'd never make it," Mallory told him. "I'd cut you down before you made Step One."

"Ha! Don't you think I know about you, cop? You ain't never killed anybody in yer whole cop career. So, ya see, I ain't all that concerned."

"What do you call the bullets I threw at you, then? Butterflies?"

"You weren't aimin' at me — just shootin'."

That was true. But he'd been shooting to get him to back off and stop shooting, to prevent him harming the little girl.

"Are you afraid you're gonna hurt me with your little bullets, Mallory?" McKenzie mocked him. "Don't you know you can't hurt me? I'm special! I'm like – charmed."

"Whatever. You've butchered your last human being, McKenzie. I won't let go of you."

"How can you hold somethin' you can't catch? Nobody's never touched me. I touch them. It gets me off, you know, caressing them with my knife, watching their blood run smooth and quick across their naked skin like spilled red paint. Did you know blood sounds just like rain if you sprinkle enough of it on the floor?"

The oddly poetic tone in the killer's voice made Mallory's gut sicken all the more. McKenzie must have sensed it, for he started to chuckle, low and deep, and it rose in his throat like an approaching semi-trailer until it burst upon Mallory's ears with a roar that reverberated throughout the house.

Despite himself, Mallory shivered. He rubbed his hand over his face and combed his fingers through his hair. Suddenly he remembered the little girl. She was curled up into a tight little ball, leaning against his kidneys. He reached his hand around and patted her back.

"Everything's gonna be all right, Samantha," he whispered. "I won't let him hurt your mommy."

She made a whining noise in her throat as she nodded, trusting him. He hoped he wouldn't let her down.

He began to examine the room more closely, looking for something, anything, to give him an edge. It crept across his mind that he could just open up and start shooting, and blow the interior of the farmhouse to bits, taking McKenzie with it. He had enough ammunition to probably get him, but how much did McKenzie have? He couldn't chance drawing that kind of assault on himself with the girl there.

A familiar dark shape on the floor a few feet toward the window caught his eyes. Easing the girl to the side, he stretched out low and grasped it silently. Recoiling to his squat, he examined the thing. It was a toy gun.

"That's my cousin Jimmy's," Samantha whispered. "He must've forgot it."

Mallory hefted the toy in his hand — it had a fair weight for a toy pistol. It was a copy of the very gun he carried, a little smaller, lighter, of course, but still very similar. It was metal, save for the handgrip, which was plastic. The fragment of an idea flittered into his mind. He caught it, built on it. It might work.

"Whatcha doin', cop?" came McKenzie's voice suddenly. "Ain't heard a peep outa you fer awhile! Have ya died of fright?"

"Don't bet on it," Mallory told him.

"Good, good. I want you alive when I carve you up. It's no fun if yer already dead." McKenzie chuckled low and deep. "You know what the best part is, cop? When I cut off pieces of them and show 'em what I took from 'em. They really like that. Some of 'em even stop yellin' and stare at it, like they can't believe that part of 'em is floatin' free in my hand. An artist needs that feedback from the people, ya know?" He laughed then, that high, shrieking, kiddie-laugh again. "That's what your brother did, ya know. He stared with his eyes popped wide open. I did him last. He got to watch me do the other one first. You shoulda seen that boy sweat! Didn't scream, though. The first one was screamin' long before I even touched him. Yer brother, though, he kept tellin' me how I'd never get away with it." He laughed. "Funny, all you cops say that when yer down to yer last pitch. He kept tellin' me about you and how you'd get me for this. Wanna know how I did him? I took one finger at a time to start with. He didn't start screamin' until I took his arm off. Then I wanted to make rain with it, so I hadda shut him up. Cut his tongue off and stuffed some parts in his mouth – don't even know if they were his!"

McKenzie's cackle made Mallory shiver. His innards felt like they were trying to turn him inside out. He didn't want to, but he kept picturing Ted in his mind, poor Ted while McKenzie was ... 'doing him'. *My God, why Ted? Why anybody?*

"Now it's your turn, cop, pig, Mr. Police Detective! I think I'll keep your head. Your brother figgered you were so great, I think I better make you a trophy — show how great you're not! So come on, pig! I'm gettin' bored! Come on out and get slaughtered! I wanna hear you squeal!"

Two bullets tore through the back of the couch with a roar, one crashing through the window, the other imbedding itself in the wall. Mallory felt the rush of that one past his forehead.

He signaled the girl to lie flat.

"Please don't let him hurt my mommy," she pleaded. "Please."

"I won't. I promise." He let the tremor in his gut come up his throat, let it be heard in his voice. "All right, McKenzie, I'll make you a deal. I'll give myself up to you if you let the lady and the child go."

"Forget it!"

Damn it.

"You're just about done in anyway, cop. I can hear it in your voice. Have you pissed yerself yet?"

"Come on, McKenzie. You know both of us aren't leaving here alive, not if you keep this up."

"That's the way I want it, stupid. I want you."

"I ain't done in yet!" he called back, hoping for a false note of bravado in his voice.

"Ha! You can't get outa here alive — you just said it yerself. You can't make it to the door. You only got in 'cause I let you in. You can't even get through that window behind you – I'd blow you in half before you could even cut yerself."

"But then you'd have nothing left to carve up. Wouldn't that spoil your fun?"

There was silence for a moment. "I'd still have the lady. Not interested in the kid. Either way, you're a stuck pig." He shrieked with laughter. Then he fired four bullets at the couch, spewing tufts of stuffing into the air that settled on Mallory and the girl.

As soon as he was sure McKenzie had pulled the trigger enough to suit him, Mallory took advantage of his own raging emotions. He gathered them, made them perform for him.

"All right!" His voice actually cracked in his dry throat. "All right! I shoulda known I couldn't beat you! Come and get me and get it over with!"

Samantha raised her head and stared at him. He couldn't see her expression, but he could feel her terror. He crossed his fingers and held them close to her face so she could see he was gambling. She lay her head back down on her arms.

"Come on, McKenzie! Just do me first so I don't have to watch you do the others! I couldn't stand that!"

He heard McKenzie chuckle that deep, bull-throated chuckle.

"Throw out yer gun first."

"All right — okay." Mallory twisted carefully around the edge of the couch and estimated the distance. Weighing the toy again in his hand, he drew back and sent it skidding across the hardwood floor. It came to a halt in the center of the floor, half way between himself and McKenzie. He prayed to God McKenzie wouldn't realize that it sounded too light to be real.

The sinister snicker that seeped out of McKenzie's lips gave Mallory a jolt of hope. His eyes riveted on the doorway, he saw McKenzie's towering shadow come out from behind the wall. It paused briefly, looking for the gun, then moved forward slowly. Mallory saw McKenzie's revolver still held ready.

"Heh-heh. Your little brother would be disappointed in you, Mallory. You just let him down."

Mallory drew himself back silently, like a snake, and crouched behind the end of the couch, drawing a bead on McKenzie as the giant bent over to pick up the toy. Before he could touch it, Mallory told him.

"Freeze right there, McKenzie."

McKenzie's big boulder of a head lifted and he looked toward Mallory without straightening up, his thick fingers wavering over the toy gun. He saw the detective's arms balanced on the back of the couch, the .357 Magnum in both hands, balanced for deadly accuracy. He couldn't miss.

"What're you tryin' to pull?" he growled.

"The plug, McKenzie. Your plug. Drop the gun."

"What, this?" He waggled his pistol in his fingers, as if it was all just a game. He stretched down a fraction more for the toy.

"Don't," Mallory warned him. "That one won't do you any good anyway."

"Oh, no?" He made as if to grab it but brought up the real one and fired at Mallory. Mallory pulled his own trigger at almost the same second. Both of them went flying backwards.

Samantha screamed as Mallory tumbled nearly on top of her. He grabbed for her shoulder, held her down with his left arm. The flesh of his bicep was burning with the graze it had taken. He knew there was a gouge right into the muscle, but that was lucky — damned lucky.

He sprang back up and looked for McKenzie. The behemoth was sprawled back against the wall. Mallory could hear his breath coming in heaves. He checked for the guns — both were lying only inches from each other, and well out of McKenzie's reach. Cautiously, he rose to his feet, keeping his muzzle zeroed in on McKenzie.

"The knife, McKenzie. Take it out real slow and slide it over to me."

"Fuck you."

"Now, McKenzie." What light there was coming in the window gave him the briefest glimpse of steel as McKenzie pulled out his carving knife.

"Come'n get it, pig."

"Put it on the floor."

"No."

"On the floor."

"No."

"You're done in, McKenzie. Give it up and we'll get you to a hospital."

"So some quack can practice his art on me? No fuckin' way. Besides, nobody takes my knife that easy, cop. You want it, come'n get it."

Damn it. Now what? Did he just shoot him dead and take him that way? Not if he didn't have to. But he wasn't going anywhere near that knife while McKenzie was still holding onto it.

He stepped sideways to his left, toward the telephone stand near the hall entrance. It was probably useless, but he picked up the receiver anyway and held it to his ear. Dead.

McKenzie snickered.

Mallory shifted over to face him squarely again. "I know I hit you in the chest," he said. "You don't have long if you don't get help."

A chuckle rumbled in McKenzie's throat. "Does that bother you, little cop? Are you afraid you've killed me?" He laughed, tossing his head back, thumping it against the wall. "You have to, if you want my knife. 'Cause I ain't goin' in. Either I die, or you die." McKenzie paused, shifting his body awkwardly. "I know that you're here alone ... No back-up comin' fer a long time. Maybe never. You can't get me outa here without help."

Mallory knew he was right. Even if he did get the knife, what did he do with him then? Send the kid down to free her mother and get to a neighbor's. He turned his head over his shoulder to speak to Samantha when suddenly McKenzie struggled to rise. Mallory faced him squarely and leveled his gun at his chest.

"Sit back down."

Grunting, holding his left hand against his lower right ribs, McKenzie got to his feet. He held the knife out with his right hand.

"Drop it," Mallory commanded. "I *will* shoot you."

"Ha! You're too soft, Mallory. You don't like to hurt things, even big mean things like me."

"You're carryin' one slug already," Mallory reminded him, however needlessly. He backed a step from the towering man.

"If you're gonna do it, do it now." McKenzie slid one foot toward him.

"Last chance, McKenzie — back off."

McKenzie chuckled and waved the knife at him. "Kill me, cop — kill me, cop," he chanted.

Behind him, still on the floor behind the couch, Samantha whimpered. Mallory's head turned toward the sound. McKenzie lunged and Mallory reacted, pulling the trigger and blowing the knife out of his hand and a hole into that hand at the wrist.

McKenzie roared in pain and shock. He coddled the useless hand, groaning and rocking it as his own blood poured out of the eaves trough of his arm. He turned round, unbelieving eyes on Mallory.

"What have you done to me? That was my hand! My good working artist's hand! I can't work left-handed!" He stumbled around, looking for the knife, but it was in fragments amongst the blood drops on the floor.

He faced Mallory again. Roaring in mad outrage, he charged the detective. Mallory fired again and he knew the bullet went right through McKenzie. The giant fell upon him, pushing him backwards over the couch, crushing him.

Upside-down, Mallory still had a hold of his gun. Samantha had screamed and he could hear her scrambling back toward the window. McKenzie loomed above him, grabbing at him. Mallory couldn't move, jammed as he was with his back on the seat, his head hanging over the edge, his legs up over the back of the couch and pinned beneath McKenzie's weight. He was half-expecting the huge man to start breaking him up; his whole body was ready for the first bone to snap. He couldn't shoot from this position without taking part of his own leg off. He felt the rough, exposed bone of McKenzie's wrist brush his arm, leaving a sticky wet trail of blood up to his hand.

Then McKenzie's good hand closed over both of his and the gun. Mallory couldn't believe it as he saw his hands so dwarfed. McKenzie's squeezed, like a vise. Mallory pulled and twisted but he couldn't get out of the deadly grip. His finger couldn't get from around the guard to the trigger.

Now it comes, he thought. *Now he starts bending my fingers back and snapping them one by one.* He tried to kick and wrench himself free but he was firmly stuck.

McKenzie began to chuckle, a very low, victorious chuckle. He stared down into Mallory's eyes and grinned, his face oddly aglow in the light of the rising sun. Mallory stared back, for the first time tonight seeing the absolute madness in McKenzie's eyes. Mallory had looked into eyes before — eyes that despised him, eyes that feared him and what he stood for, eyes that glinted that they were going to kill him. But McKenzie's eyes were something else entirely. They were windows to Hell with the shades all the way up, and when Mallory looked in, he saw the twisted, pulsing snarl of blackness that was McKenzie's soul.

His breath caught in his throat. He wasn't a man prone to gasping aloud or screaming, but he almost did. His gut knotted in revulsion at what he saw and again he fought to get free.

Abruptly McKenzie hauled on his captured hands and pulled him off the seat cushion, suspending Mallory in mid-air. McKenzie's fingers pried at his, loosening them from the grips. Mallory set his jaw, trying to hold onto the gun. If McKenzie wanted it, he was going to have to break his fingers to get it.

Mallory's body jerked in shock as McKenzie took his right index finger and inserted it through the semi-circle of the trigger guard.

My God, he's gonna make me pull the trigger on myself, Mallory thought as McKenzie's hand tightened over his as firmly as before. To be out-muscled by this behemoth was one thing, but to have to let him kill him with his own gun, his own finger. To leave this mother and child with no one to protect them.

"Damn it!" he shouted, his whole body fit to explode with frustration. He resisted as McKenzie raised the gun from between Mallory's knees. He might as well have tried to resist the force of gravity. His hands surrounded the gun but McKenzie controlled it. It lifted and Mallory could only watch, waiting, waiting for it to turn on him and blow him into the next world.

But his arms remained straight and Mallory was staring down the barrel at McKenzie's face, just as if he were sighting him by himself. For one split second, he saw the intention in McKenzie's eyes, and then his finger was pressed into the trigger. There was a deafening explosion and he was suddenly free.

His torso bounced lightly on the seat cushion. His gun was still in his hands. The ringing in his ears was Samantha shrieking somewhere behind him. Swinging his feet to the floor, he went to her, his head swimming for the moments it took to settle her down. Then he left her and walked to the other side of the couch. What was left of McKenzie was sprawled, quite dead, in the middle of the hardwood floor.

THE CAMAS FAIRY

A chilly mist shrouded the entrance to the pathway at the foot of Bear Hill. The paved corridor of Brookleigh Road was silent this early in the morning. Dale crossed it and stepped into the forest on the other side.

Witch's hair lichen draped from old maples. A raven called *'chuk-a-luck, chuk-a-luck'* as it swooshed through the branches above Dale and settled high in a Douglas fir. Sunlight slipped in thin streams through the mist, illuminating the understory of salal, Oregon grape, and sword ferns. He hoped the sun would not burn away the otherworldly mist just yet.

A faint breeze fluttered foliage. Insects flittered in his peripheral vision. He breathed the scent of leaf litter decomposing into the damp soil. The trail steepened. Dale's eyes felt caressed by each familiar tree, rock, and twist in the trail. Higher, the forest changed, and groves of arbutus and Garry oaks thrived. He scowled at the cell tower and the new homes that had crept too high up the hill. Finding his old route, he left the main trail and tread on soft moss and green grass.

Wildflowers greeted him—bright bluebells and nodding pink shooting stars. He crossed the open rocky meadow to gaze south over Elk and Beaver Lakes toward the city of Victoria, BC. Southward beyond the small city rose the Olympic Mountains of Washington State, the Strait of Juan de Fuca shimmering between. To the east, Mount Baker's ever-snowy peak glowed in the orange sunrise. Dale's gaze drew back across the islands dotting Haro Strait, along sweeping farmland, and up to his rugged sanctuary. This had always been home. Always would be.

A bald eagle soared along a thermal above him as the sun burned off the last of the mist. Small birds twittered in the bushes. He crossed the meadow and ventured down the crevice in the rock face on the other side, careful not to disturb the moss and tear it from its purchase.

The patch of camas was exactly where it was each year, its starry blue flowers waving to him in the breeze. The plant had been of great importance to the native peoples in days gone by. They had owned and tended great fields of camas, digging the bulbs and cooking them for days until they were sweet. But only the blue ones. The white-flowered camas they called the Death Camas. They would dig them up and destroy them. There were three white camas plants amongst the blue. Normally, Dale would never consider disturbing wild plants, especially in a park. He pulled the trowel from his jacket pocket and dug up the three white plants. He'd read that all parts of the plant were poisonous. Leaves, flowers, bulbs. And bitter as they would be, he would eat all three raw.

He carried them to the mossy rock ledge he used to hide out on as a boy. Overhung with cedar bows, it was smaller than he recalled. He crawled beneath the bows and sat cross-legged within their shelter. Laying the plants on the moss before him, he chose one and sunk his teeth into the bulb. Its acrid taste twisted his face in disgust, but he chewed the tough plant until he had eaten the whole thing. He ate the second, all the while fighting the urge to retch. He wasn't certain from his hasty research how long it would take for the neurotoxins to take effect or how much was enough. He would devour all three. He wasn't looking forward to the nausea, dizziness, ataxia, and eventual heart failure, but soon there would be coma and death, and that would be appropriate. He picked up the third white camas.

"You're not going to eat any more, are you?"

Dale dropped the plant and peered around for the tiny familiar voice.

"I've been waiting for your return—but not to do something so foolish."

"My return?" Dale twisted left and right, trying to locate the speaker. "And you don't know anything about why—. Who are you? Where are you?"

"I am Harrier. You used to call me Harry. And I'm over here."

Dale followed the flicker in the corner of his eye, and there on a leathery salal leaf stood Harrier, shimmering an iridescent dragonfly blue.

"You're real? I thought I'd imagined you!"

"Most adults convince themselves of that."

Though childhood memories parted his lips with a smile, Dale's head slumped to his chest and he sighed from deep in his soul. "It's been such a long time." He tipped his face toward Harrier. "I've failed, you know. I did as you asked me so long ago. I went to university. I studied botany and forest biology and the Druids and Tree Lore and Fairy Lore and all those other things you said I would need to know so I could help. So others would take me seriously when I tried to help." Dale shook his head. "But none of it helped. No one really listened. Those that pretended to are all saying I'm '*a little off*'. Oh, not to my face, mind you. They're very kind to my face." Dale stopped himself and spit out a stray fiber of camas. "The point is that no matter what I do, they won't stop. They keep destroying the forests, building roads and houses where they don't belong. They don't want to know the truth, because then they would have to stop and not make so much of their precious money." Dale's head wobbled and his shoulders shook as he began to sob. "I failed. I couldn't change anything."

"I know you tried. We all do. The world of men is evolving, but with excruciating slowness. We can only keep trying to reach them. Many are beginning to awaken."

Dale's hand reached toward Harrier in a helpless gesture and then fell to the moss with a gentle thud.

"But for you, it is time to choose. If you choose to live, you must come with me." Harry's dragonfly wings quivered.

Dale blinked away his tears, rubbed his blurry eyes with the backs of his hands. "Where?"

Harry took flight from the salal leaf and flitted down the rock ledge. Dale's eyes followed him, and suddenly the rock slope revealed itself to be rough-hewn stone steps leading down to a grassy meadow, in the center of which stood an ancient and massive Garry oak tree, its branches twisted in beautiful knurls and covered in moss and lichen. Around the base of the tree was a bright ring of white mushrooms. Dale stumbled down the steps. He was losing motor control. It was hard to breath.

"If I come with you, I can't ever come back, can I?"

"If you don't eat or drink anything while you're with us, you can return."

Dale smiled and stepped into the fairy ring. "Lead me to the feast, my friend!"

THE CHURCHYARD INCIDENT

Mist gathered in the fields as Freddie stepped off the paved road onto the long gravel drive. Loose stones crunched and rolled under his sneakers. Warm yellow light invited him through the dusk to the farmhouse ahead, but the narrow driveway was fringed with shadowed scrub and ancient oaks that reached for him with gnarled, bare autumn branches.

A breeze brushed his left shoulder, then dropped to worry dry leaves along the ground. Something rustled in the brush and Freddie skipped aside, his eyes fixed on the darkest shadow they found.

'*A rabbit,*' he thought. '*A rabbit.*' The rustling ceased. He carried on, hating the noisy gravel — he'd never hear anything coming over his own footsteps. Reaching the front porch, he knocked, and glanced around. Thick mist appeared caught in the woods beyond the house. It tore away, reaching for the house — and him — like fingers of rent vaporous wool. A moth fluttered against the porch light. Freddie heard someone running thump-thump-thump across the hardwood floors inside the house. The runner's feet skidded to a halt and their owner flung open the door.

"Freddie!"

Freddie's apprehensions vanished the second he saw Rand, who grabbed his thin arm and yanked him inside. Freddie giggled.

"Man, Freddie," Rand said, "You gotta do somethin' about that hair of yours."

Freddie's eyes followed Rand's gaze to the hall mirror where, by some queer trick of reflection, the porch light behind him seemed to set Freddie's red hair into a halo of fire.

Rand slammed the door. "Come on — Chris's already here."

"Who's —?"

Rand pulled him into the living room without giving him a chance to take off his shoes. "Freddie's here!"

Heat burned Freddie's cheeks as he stood before his friend's parents, both seated in cozy armchairs. On the pine table between them, two cups of tea steamed on a white doily.

"Hello, Freddie," said Rand's mom, setting her crocheting on her lap. "Nice to see you again."

Rand's dad shook his paper and peered over it. "Hello, son."

"H-hello —." Freddie's eyes skipped across the strange boy sitting silently in the wooden chair in the corner.

"That's Chris." Rand leaned his forearm on Freddie's narrow shoulder. "This is my best buddy, Freddie."

A smile erupted from Freddie's face. He was Rand's best buddy.

Rand's mom remarked: "You boys must have seen each other on the road and not known you were both headed here. Chris arrived only a few moments before you."

Chris rose and approached Rand and Freddie. His mouth quirked in what might have been a smile. A lock of his straight black hair fell over his round black eyes. He flicked it back with a jerk of his head.

"Hey, kid."

"H-hi."

"Listen to Chris's deep voice!" said Rand's mom. "He sounds so much older than the other two."

Rand's dad grunted agreeably.

Rand shook Freddie's shoulders. "Come on — we're outta here." He steered Freddie toward the back door. "Remember, Mom!" he called over his shoulder. "No coming out to check up on us!"

"Yes, dear."

The back porch was buried under a pile of camping gear. They all grabbed some and hauled it to the center of the big back yard. They worked quickly in the fading light, setting up the tent, unrolling sleeping bags. When Freddie fumbled with one of the hooks, Rand took it from him and snapped it deftly into place.

Shrugging, Freddie smiled. "Thanks." Then he blushed as he realized Chris was watching.

At last, they stood back and observed their encampment. Rand had stripped down to his white T-shirt, having worked up a sweat pumping up the air mattresses. Glowing like the rising three-quarter moon, he stepped forward with a kingly bearing and shouted for the stars to hear:

"I declare this a good camp!"

Freddie sucked air through his mouth and tried to think of something to add.

Rand's bright grin interrupted him. "I gotta take a leak." He pivoted and trotted off toward the back fence. Freddie raised a hand to point at the back door of the house.

Chris crossed his arms in front of his chest. "You don't go in to use the toilet when you're camping, Carrot-Top."

Cold hurt stiffened Freddie's heart at even so old and empty an insult. He turned away from Chris and followed the path Rand had pressed in the damp grass. He didn't have to go, but he had to get away from Chris.

"Hey, man," Rand greeted him over his shoulder.

"Hey."

"What's with you, man? Did you get bad news from the doc this afternoon?"

"No." He turned and glanced at the boy near the tent. "I — I guess I kind of figured it would just be you and me for camping." He brushed his foot through the grass.

"Oh. Well, it was gonna be, but then they brought this new kid in after you left, and I figured he was okay, so I invited him to come along. The more the merrier, right?"

"I — I guess."

"So come on — loosen up. It's gonna be great!" With that, Rand howled at the moon and sprang off racing in circles around the yard.

Freddie watched him, wishing he could be inside Rand's skin, feel that life energy rushing and sparking. Already handsome at fourteen, perfectly proportioned in muscle and bone, Rand had never had an awkward stage and probably never would. The girls at school already whispered and giggled over him — a very different kind of giggling than when they saw Freddie.

"Come on, Freddie!" Rand yelled, waving.

Freddie scuffed through the damp grass and crawled into the tent after Rand and Chris. A propane lamp glared a harsh white light from the center of the tent. It swung a bit as he fidgeted to get comfortable on his air mattress.

"So, whadayou guys wanna do?" asked Rand, pulling on his plaid flannel shirt. "Wanna tell ghost stories?"

"Yeah," Chris agreed. He shook his dark hair out of his eyes and looked at Freddie.

"That all right with you, kid?"

"'Course it's all right," Freddie said, trying to answer the way he figured Rand would. Halloween wasn't really until next Thursday, but their parents wouldn't let them camp out on a school night so they were having their last camping night of the year tonight, the Saturday before Halloween.

"Freddie's no weenie," Rand declared, smacking the redhead's knee. "He's just been sick a lot. It ain't his fault."

Freddie's cheeks heated and his normally almost translucent skin glowed to rival his freckles. He ducked his head after a grateful glance at his friend.

"If you say so," Chris said. "But I bet he was thinking that it's not Halloween yet — as if that's a good enough excuse not to tell ghost stories." He stared at Freddie, his dark eyes glittering with smug shrewdness.

A tremor rippled in Freddie's belly. He crossed his arms in front of himself and broke the gaze with Chris. He flushed again. How had Chris known that?

Suddenly Freddie recoiled as Chris lunged toward him. Chris's hand clamped on his shoulder and Freddie wished he could dissolve through the nylon membrane of the tent and run away.

"It never has to be Halloween for ghost stories," Chris said, his face too close to Freddie's. "Any time of the year will do.

It's just that at this time of the year, those who know say that the veil between the worlds grows thin, and it's easier for spirits to cross back and forth."

"Yeah," Rand chimed in. "It only gots to be dark and spooky. Like tonight."

"Well, it makes for a nice touch," Chris agreed, amusement quirking the corner of his mouth. "Evil lurks at every moment. It can manifest anytime, anywhere, any way. And you'll never know just how — at least not until it's too late." He paused, then began to chant: "Evil comes in many guises; different shapes and different sizes."

Rand caught on immediately and chanted in time with Chris: "Evil comes in many guises; different shapes and different sizes. Evil comes in many guises; different shapes and different sizes!"

They sprang at Freddie and grabbed him. Freddie shrieked, half from fright, half from Chris's painful grip. Chris's fingers were like sharp sticks, poking into his flesh. Freddie barely noticed Rand was tickling him and laughing.

"Ow! Let go!"

Chris and Rand reared back and raised their arms above their heads like monster claws.

"We're gonna get you!"

"No!" Freddie shrank back against the tent wall.

They began the chant again, over and over until Freddie was cringing in the corner, his palms pressed tight over his ears. "Stop it! Don't say that!" A sob escaped his tight throat.

"Aw, give it up," Chris said, dropping back on his own sleeping bag. "Before he pees himself and brings the whole tent down on us. What a wimp."

Rand kneeled next to Freddie. "They're just words, Fred. They don't mean nothin'."

"Yes, they do," Freddie blubbered. "They're evil words. They mean —."

Chris guffawed. "What do they mean, kid? They mean the boogieman's gonna get you?"

Freddie choked, trying to sit up and recover himself, explain what he felt about the words. But he didn't know if it was the words themselves or Chris's voice, which seemed so much older than his and Rand's, so much older than anything. Freddie heard something in those words, in that voice. Usually he could make a picture in his head that helped him explain strange things to himself, but he couldn't see anything that made any sense this time. "Maybe. I don't know. But —."

"But, schmut. And you're right — you don't know. So quit being such a wimp."

Rand lightly punched Freddie's shoulder. "You okay now, Fred?"

Freddie nodded and sniffled. He hoped he hadn't embarrassed Rand by being such a baby in front of his new friend. He rubbed his neck where Chris had dug his fingers in deep. He cast a glance and saw Chris watching him.

Rand flipped onto his back and hollered, pumping his arms and legs in the air as if he were running. "Hey, look, Freddie! I'm goin' nowhere fast!"

They all laughed. Freddie wiped his eyes on his sleeve.

"You plan to win that race on Monday?" Chris asked Rand.

"You bet!"

"You're the best runner on the team."

Rand grinned.

"I'm coming to watch!" Freddie promised. "I'll cheer and everything!"

"Cool."

Chris drew up his knees, draping his forearms over them. "You're a real pal, aren't you, Carrot-Top?"

Crimson burned Freddie's ears.

Rand quit his mock running and let his feet drop to the mattress with twin thumps. "Don't call him that. He hates it."

"Sorry, Ran-man." Chris looked around the tent like he was bored. Then he said, "Come on — let's do the ghost stories. Did you hear the one about the Specter Axe Man?"

"Yep."

"What about the Hounds from Hell?"

"A gazillion times."

Sighing heavily, Chris appeared to think a moment. Freddie hoped he wouldn't come up with anything.

"What about the one with the kid who disappears in the churchyard?"

"Uh, nope," answered Rand. "You hear that one, Fred?"

Freddie shook his head.

"Okay, then, this is it," Chris declared. He wriggled on his mattress, getting comfortable. "It happens in a little town like this one. There's this old church on the edge of town, where nobody goes anymore."

"Is there a graveyard?" asked Rand, leaning toward him.

"Yeah. All old and busted headstones and stuff."

"Cool!"

His voice thin and tentative, Freddie asked, "What kinda church is it?"

Chris scowled at him. "Whadaya mean, what kinda church is it? It's just a church."

"It might be important."

"It's not. Any stupid old church'll do."

"Think of the old Crossroads Church, on the way to the gravel pits," Rand suggested.

"Anyway," Chris continued, a wicked gleam glazing his dark eyes. "One day, outa nowhere, comes this old man. He's really, really old with pure white hair. He doesn't talk much to adults — only to kids. The kids really like him. He's always got great stories for them. One kid especially, Timmy, hangs out with him a lot."

"What do they do?" Freddie asked, getting curious.

"Just take walks in the forest and talk about stuff. The old guy tells Timmy lots of stories. One day he tells him about the time he was the caretaker of the church in his hometown, and one night he was out there late and he saw this kid running around the church backwards. He said the kid ran around three times and then right before his eyes — just vanished."

Rand straightened up. "Get outa here!"

"True story. And then Timmy wanted to find out if it was true or not, so he ran around the church three times backwards and he disappeared, too."

"No way!"

"True story," Chris repeated, nodding.

Freddie cleared his throat timidly. "Where did they disappear to?"

"The Other Side."

"Of the church?"

"No. Of the spirit world. Where demons rule."

Dark things sprinted behind Freddie's mind's eye and he shuddered. "Did — did they die?"

"No. They'll never die. They're still alive, being tormented by the demons."

"What do the d-demons do to them?"

"Terrible things. Awful things. Dark things. You couldn't take it, Freddie."

"Can they ever get out and come back?"

"No. Never."

"But they were good kids, weren't they? Why did they have to end up there?"

"It doesn't matter if they're good. It's their destiny." Chris turned a cock-eyed grin on him. "But they take bad people, too, to work for them and catch the good ones for the demons to play with. In exchange, the demons won't torture them. Unless they screw up."

Freddie wrapped his thin arms around his knees and pulled them into his chest, trying to fend off a chill colder than the damp night air that was seeping into his flesh, poking his insides, seeking his bones. The three of them sat in death-like silence. Then Rand began to chuckle and finally burst out laughing.

"Freddie — you should see yourself! You're whiter than usual!"

Freddie flushed, crimson staining his pale cheeks, creeping into his scalp, and blending with his flaming hair under the glare of the propane lamp.

Chris appeared to be looking right through the roof of the blue nylon tent. "The moon's rising."

Rand sucked in a deep breath and howled like a forlorn wolf.

Freddie curled into his knees, his forearms pressing over his ears. "Don't, Rand, please!"

"Aw, you ain't scared again are you?"

Freddie lifted his head tentatively. "A — a little."

"It's just a stupid story."

"I — I know. I mean I don't know."

"Well, know."

"Why don't you go try it," Chris suggested. "Then if you disappear you'll know for sure." He chuckled derisively.

"No way!"

"Sure, Freddie," Rand said. "I'll even do it with you."

Freddie shook his head emphatically. "Uh-uh."

"Come on — it'll be a blast!"

"No! I don't wanna disappear and get tortured by demons!" He grabbed the edges of his sleeping bag and wrapped them around himself.

Chris muttered some curse out the side of his mouth. He shook his head at Rand. "How did you ever pick this weenie for a best friend?"

"Shut up." Rand cocked his head and studied Freddie's face.

Freddie was afraid and he knew he couldn't hide it from Rand.

"Well, Freddie, there's only one way to fix this." Rand crawled the foot or so to the doorway and unzipped the tent flap. "Let's go."

Freddie blinked at him. "Go where?"

"To the old church. I'll run around it backwards and you can see it's just a story and you won't have to be scared anymore."

Cold fire seared through Freddie's chest. "No! You don't have to. I'm not going!"

"Then stay here and Chris'll come with me to prove I did it." He waved his arm and Chris crawled in front of Freddie and followed Rand out into the night.

"Wait! Don't! What if it's for real? Rand!" He heard their footsteps receding through the grass, their voices drifting away. "Wait! Don't leave me here alone!"

"Then come on!"

Freddie hesitated a moment longer. The glare of the propane lamp was no comfort when even his shadow was alone on the blue tent lining. Suddenly realizing he could no longer hear the other boys, he gathered his sleeping bag securely around his shoulders and plunged through the sliver of an opening into the blackness of the world outside.

Momentarily blind, he stumbled in a circle before finding his bearings in the feeble light of the low moon. He set off after them, but paused at the house and gazed up at the warm yellow light in the windows.

"Shouldn't we tell —?"

He left off, knowing they were too far away to hear him. He hustled out to the end of the driveway, hating every noisy, crunchy step. He peered down the black top, but they were already out of sight. The damp road was a silvery incision between the forest and the fields. He looked again, both ways, hoping he'd just missed their silhouettes in the mist.

Maybe they were hiding. "Come out, you guys!" Holding his breath, he listened. Nothing but the flutter of tiny creatures hiding in the brush. Nothing human. Not even a giggle. "Where are you?"

An urgent autumn breeze pressed at his back and he started walking. The old church was just over a mile away, around the corner. They couldn't be that far yet. He ran a few yards, then, out of breath, fell back. He'd never catch up.

Then he remembered the trail that cut through the woods and came out at the church's back yard. That would save him time! He hurried forward again, only to come up short when he found the path. The old boards across the ditch were gone. It was nearly two yards across. There was cold, dark water in the ditch. The path was a black hole in the trees on the other side.

"Afraid of the dark, Carrot-Top?"

Freddie spun around to face Chris, his heart leaping into his throat, thumping painfully. His eyes searched the darkness. "Where's Rand?"

"Halfway to his destiny."

"What do you mean?"

"We all reach our destiny, some sooner, some later. Some even share a common one. All are inescapable. Perhaps yours is to save Rand from the one I have chosen for him. Perhaps not." Chris grinned.

In all his life of being teased and taunted, Freddie had never seen a grin drip with so much malice. He looked around again for Rand. Chris chuckled, then laughed, then vanished.

Freddie gasped, stepped back. Chris was gone! And Chris was … He didn't know what Chris was, but whatever he was, he was evil. A sudden weakness quivered in Freddie's stomach and knees. He tottered on the pavement, rocked by the sudden birth of his unexplainable fears into reality.

He had to get to Rand. Stop him from doing whatever it was Chris wanted him to do.

Somewhere in the distance the wind gathered and with a strange, un-wind like roar rushed toward him, ripping at the trees and tearing at the sleeping bag around his shoulders. He clutched the bag tightly, refusing to let go though it whipped and flapped about him, one corner stinging him in the eye. He leaned into the wind, his eyes squinted nearly shut, tears streaming from them. He took one step, then another. The seconds he balanced on one foot seemed eons while the other made its gambit for the next piece of earth. He wasn't even sure he was headed for the ditch anymore. Then suddenly the wind stopped. Freddie could not breathe in the vacuum that encapsulated him. His heart pounded madly in his chest until at last his lungs drew air. Panting, bent over his knees, he focused on the trail once again. Chris was new in town — he couldn't know about the path.

Freddie wished he had a flashlight. He judged the distance across the ditch, backed up, and took a run at it. He leapt and landed hard on the other side, his hands grabbing for any purchase on the earth, his feet slipping and splashing into the cold muck of the ditch. His soaked sleeping bag seemed to suck him back deeper into the mire. Slithering out from under it, he scrambled up the bank.

He'd never taken the path in the dark before, nor ever taken it alone. Rand had always been with him. The soft dirt was dampened by the autumn rains but not yet saturated into mud. Some portions were slick with old fallen leaves, while in the more sheltered spots the leaves were still crunchy beneath his feet.

A searching breeze rustled the few remaining leaves overhead. The thin bare branches scratched and scraped against each other like dried-up finger bones. Freddie moved on.

The path became darker and darker as he moved deeper into the forest. He stepped cautiously, his hands spread before him in the black void. He stumbled over a root and fell, the earth an invisible barrier that stopped his fall into nothing. He wondered if the wind would descend upon him now and finish him off.

Suddenly he thought he heard voices. Pushing himself to his feet, he trekked forward, more careful of roots and rocks now. Moments later, he emerged at the edge of the church's back yard. He scanned the clearing between himself and the whitewashed church, but saw no one.

The small clapboard church seemed incandescent in the wan light of the mist and moon. An historical landmark, the church had stood on this spot for a hundred and forty years. It appeared sturdy, but hadn't been structurally sound for years.

Freddie's eyes searched the churchyard, examining the precise black shadows of the pine trees dotting the unkempt lawn and the headstones crouching just beyond them.

"We gotta wait for Freddie, so he can see." Rand's voice carried across the empty air.

Freddie saw them now, silhouetted against the pale gravel driveway. "Hey, Freddie!" called Rand, waving. Freddie waved back, his voice squeezed silent though he wanted to call out so desperately in relief.

Then he felt Chris's eyes on him and the breeze became wind as it skimmed low through the mist, across the grass, and shoved his feet out from under him.

He landed hard in the turf, losing the air in his lungs with a grunt. The ground was wet and cold and quickly soaked his clothes. The need to get to Rand overcame the chill that already stiffened his flesh. He reclaimed his breath, regained his feet, and trudged the rest of the way to the other boys.

"Where ya been?" asked Rand.

"I —."

"We thought maybe you went home or somethin'."

Freddie shook his head. "I couldn't see …" He looked from Rand to Chris.

"Well, at least you made it." Rand clapped Freddie's shoulder with an open palm. "Now you can watch, too."

Freddie's heart twisted in his chest. He started to speak but Chris cut him off.

"Let's get started."

Rand asked: "So, what do I gotta do, again?"

Chris pointed at the church. "Just run around that counter-clockwise. Three times. Backwards."

"I'm cold," Freddie asserted, trembling, his arms clutched about his thin frame. "Let's go home."

"In a minute, Freddie." Rand moved off to the southeast corner of the church.

"Don't do it!" Freddie screamed, the hysteria in his voice shocking even himself.

Chris grabbed his arm before he could run toward Rand. "You're really getting annoying, you know that?" His voice was the warning hiss of an asp and his dark eyes threatened Freddie with unveiled hostility. "Stop interfering."

Freddie shrank from Chris. "Let go!" he cried, yanking his arm free.

Chris yelled to Rand. "Go on! Get started!"

"Yeah, yeah!"

"Stop pushing him!" Freddie demanded. "You're making him do it! I know! Leave him alone!"

"You know nothing," Chris hissed back.

Neither one noticed Rand come halfway back to them. "Geez, will you guys chill out?"

Freddie spun to him, tripping over tufts of saturated grass as he tried to get to him. "Please don't do it, Rand. Chris is evil. He wants to hurt you."

Rand chuckled, his hands on his hips. "Come on, Freddie."

Freddie heard Chris coming up behind him. He was running out of time and everything he said just made both Chris and Rand more determined to take this right to the end.

"So, are we doing this?" Chris asked.

"Yeah, for sure."

"Carrot-Top whining again?" With one hand, Chris shoved Freddie so hard he stumbled backwards and nearly fell.

"Hey, take it easy!" Rand warned him. "So he's scared — in a minute I'll show him there's nothin' to be scared of." He turned and walked back toward the church.

"Rand!"

"Relax, Fred!"

"Yeah, shut up already, Carrot-Top. Or I'll hit you so hard Rand will see you cry."

Freddie wrapped his arms even more tightly around himself. The menace in Chris's voice hung in the air, writhing like a palpable, though ethereal snake.

Chris called out: "Make sure you start where I put that stick! And don't stop until you cross it after the third lap!"

"You got it!" Rand waved at them before stripping off his flannel shirt. He was easy to see now. Like the church, his white T-shirt reflected the light of the risen three-quarter moon.

Freddie focused on something mutely glowing at Rand's feet. It was Chris's marker, a broken branch long since stripped of its bark and bleached white like a bone.

"You stand here," Chris commanded Freddie. "And I'll stand on the other side to make sure he doesn't try to hide in the bushes and fool us." Chris walked away and disappeared around the far side of the church.

Freddie stood there, silent and stymied. How could he make Rand see Chris for what he was?

Warming up with jumping jacks, Rand called out: "You guys ready?"

Chris answered, "Yep!"

Freddie swallowed, trying to pop his ears. Some weird sort of pressure change had overtaken the churchyard. He suddenly felt light-headed and woozy. The earth and the air shimmered, and the night seemed somehow darker, the hovering mist more dense, yet he could still see Rand beneath the moon.

The moment Rand began to run, Freddie's eyes attached themselves to him with an umbilical-like fastness. As Rand rounded the corner to Chris's side, a sudden sweat broke out all over Freddie's body. His trembling erupted into spasms of violent shaking which he tried to contain by squeezing himself even more tightly within his own arms. When Rand came into view again, Freddie tried to cry out to him, but all that escaped was a thin, raspy nothing of sound.

Rand began his second lap. He stumbled a couple of times over uneven turf, but even backwards, he jogged with a rhythm he looked like he could maintain forever.

Freddie's pounding heart hurt more than he'd ever imagined it could. He forced himself to breathe in and out as Rand again disappeared behind the little church. He clutched his fists against his chest. The seconds crawled by, sluggishly indifferent to Freddie's dread. At last Rand appeared, swinging around the southwest corner. But there was still one more lap.

'Always the jock,' Freddie thought, knowing Rand would never go any less than all the way. He forced out a sigh, freeing the stale air trapped in his lungs. Then he sucked a deep breath through his mouth. The cold air smarted his teeth. As Rand rounded the last corner to complete his third lap, Freddie started toward him.

He watched for Chris. Sure enough, Chris came around the corner to observe Rand's finish. Freddie felt instant repulsion, but he fought the urge to run. Instead, he jumped up and down and waved at Rand. Rand waved back.

"Don't distract him!"

Freddie's eyes darted to Chris, who was striding straight toward him through the mist. Except the mist was coming before him, swirling and reaching as though propelled by an unearthly wind. Freddie stood transfixed as the first chill fingers of it reached him and coiled around him.

Suddenly Chris was in Freddie's face and Freddie couldn't block the blow to his sternum that left him on his knees in the wet grass, gasping, barely able to hear the words Chris hissed in his ear.

"I'd send you, too, just to get rid of you, if you weren't so weak! But your flimsy soul would implode and die too quickly. Rand's tough. He'll survive a long time. Maybe even forever."

Freddie's voice came out raspy. "And — and you'll hurt him forever…?"

"Not me, but the others, yes."

"I said leave him alone!"

Both Freddie and Chris looked up, startled, into Rand's furious face. Rand jabbed a finger into Chris's chest.

"I'm tellin' you for the last time to leave him alone! Stop pickin' on my buddy!"

Chris tore his eyes from Rand's to stare toward the church. "You didn't finish. You didn't cross over the stick …"

"So what? I ain't lettin' you hurt Freddie! And I ain't playin' your stupid game anymore. So just get lost!"

Chris's lip twitched and curled into a snarl. He stared hard into Rand's eyes, then into Freddie's. Freddie smiled stiffly back. Chris tensed, as though ready to strike, then pivoted and walked away.

Freddie stared after him, momentarily numb in the silence. Briefly, a cold breeze swirled around them, then was gone. Dry leaves quaked on nearby trees as Chris disappeared into the forest and the mist.

"Come on," Rand said, helping Freddie up. "Let's go home."

STABLE HANDS, STABLE HEARTS

Scott Archer tightened the cinch of his western saddle, tucked the latigo into its keeper, and let the stirrup down. Ready. He'd come last weekend as a spectator for the rodeo portion of the annual Elk Lake Fall Rodeo and Horse Show, but today he came to compete in the performance horse competitions. The last horse show of the season and if he took first place in his next class he would win the High Point trophy for the year.

Scott patted his gelding Dakota's neck and took a few long, deep breaths. "We can do this, buddy". He rechecked Dakota's gear and his own outfit. Clean and neat. Raising his eyes over the saddle, he looked across the fairgrounds, crowded with horses and riders, to see if the class currently in the ring was near to finishing.

The judge handed his decision to the announcer, who read the results over the PA.

"In First Place, Novice Western Pleasure …"

Scott's class was next — he'd better get over by the in-gate.

"Number 8, Jennifer Lo-."

A horse neighed loud and long just ten feet from Scott, drowning out the remainder of the announcement and leaving Scott's ears ringing.

Jenny? Scott's breath stuck halfway into his lungs. Had the announcer been about to say Jennifer Loewen? He strained to see through the crowd. A glimpse of the girl's face, quickly gone. He mounted Dakota, hoping the height would afford a clear view.

The rider patted her mare's neck and exited the ring with their blue ribbon. Scott stared while she maneuvered her way over to a trailer and dismounted. She lifted her white Stetson from her head and freed her brunette ponytail from her hair net.

It had to be her! But no matter how much he willed it she would not turn her face so he could see her clearly.

He started forward again, only to be cut off by a string of riders that might as well have been a mountain range. The announcer called Scott's class over the PA. He hesitated, his heart pounding in his chest. About to ditch the competition, he mentally shook himself. Probably not his Jenny. His most important class of the day — of the year — and he risked losing it to see the face of a girl he'd never even met.

Pressing his tan Stetson firmly onto his head, he reined toward the in-gate where the whipper-in checked his number and let him enter the ring. What if it was his Jenny?

Three beautiful summers they'd spent together at Cedar View Horse Camp. He recalled the day they'd met like it was yesterday. The first riding lesson of the summer. Scott had finished saddling his horse. This was all he'd ever wanted – to ride. He was saving to buy his own horse someday, and next his own stable where he would train good horses and be one of the best out there. Nothing else mattered.

Over his horse's mane, he'd spotted 10-year-old Petey struggling to wrap and knot the latigo on his pinto pony's saddle. Glancing toward the instructor, he'd seen she was busy with another first-time youngster. He'd heard Petey sniffle as the little boy's hands balled into fists at his sides.

Slipping around his mount's hindquarters, Scott had walked over, his square-toed riding boots kicking up little puffs of dust from the dry summer soil. "How's it going, Petey?"

"I can't get it," Petey admitted through clenched teeth. "I've tried a zillion times, but it won't work!"

"Let me help you. Now watch close." Scott demonstrated the wrap. After a few more tries, Petey did it by himself. "There, I knew you could do it!"

Petey smiled so big when he said 'thanks' Scott couldn't help smiling, too. He patted the younger boy on the shoulder and went back to his horse. The camp instructor, Mrs. Hogan, nodded at him, but the eyes of a girl his own age standing next to a small bay gelding made him almost walk into his buckskin's face. Petting the horse, he apologized.

Finally, they got to actually ride. Scott couldn't wait to go trail riding in the forested hills, but the new kids needed the ring, so they all started that way. The one hundred by two hundred foot riding arena felt constricting, but he forgot all about his boredom when the new girl trotted past him, her golden-brown ponytail bouncing behind her.

She smiled at him! His heart suddenly felt like it was galloping in his chest. He squeezed his mount into an extended trot to catch up to her. Settling into an easy jog-trot, he kept pace with her.

"Hi. I'm Scott."

Her big green eyes sparkled. She opened her mouth to respond, but the instructor called out commands and they had to separate and ride single file. It seemed the longest riding lesson he'd ever had. He had to content himself with watching her cute ponytail bounce in rhythm with her bum on the saddle. It looked like she'd ridden before, but not a lot.

Finally the class ended. After untacking and grooming, they led their horses out to their paddocks and turned them loose. Most of the kids were walking stiff-legged and groaning.

"That was nice, what you did, helping that little boy," she said, coming up behind him.

Scott stopped and at last gazed into her pretty face. They were the same height.

"I'm Jenny." She held out her hand.

He shook it gently and suddenly couldn't speak. Couldn't say Hi or thank her for the compliment. If he didn't come up with something fast, she might think he was rude.

Mrs. Hogan's voice rang out. "Before you all take off for your next activity, I need two volunteers to help me muck out stalls and feed and water this week."

Loud groans went up through the class, except from Scott and Jenny. Mrs. Hogan didn't seem surprised to see Scott raise his hand, but her eyes rounded a little when first-timer Jenny put her hand up simultaneously. "Thank you, Scott and Jenny. Be here at six am sharp tomorrow morning."

"Yes, Ma'am," they both replied.

The next morning Mrs. Hogan oversaw the portions of grain fed to each horse, then left Scott and Jenny with instructions for hay, turn-outs, and stall cleaning. "You'll be in good hands," she told Jenny. "Scott helps me out every summer. He was born to be around horses. I'll be in the tack room if you need me."

Scott and Jenny set to work. Together they got all the hay out to the paddocks first. He smiled to himself when she held a flake of hay to her nose and breathed in deeply. She blushed when she saw him looking at her.

"I do that all the time, too," he admitted.

They led horses out to their paddocks and filled troughs with fresh water from the hose. Scott watched her, and gave her a few tips as they went. Jenny followed his lead simply because she was green, but she seemed confident and eager to learn.

Back in the barn, he showed her how to pick the stalls clean and put in new wood shavings to keep the bedding deep.

"So, don't all the kids have to learn to muck out and stuff?" Jenny asked from her stall. She stood up and leaned on her manure fork.

"Yep. But Mrs. Hogan likes to give everybody a chance to volunteer before she starts assigning."

"I see."

"So, have you ridden much before?" he asked.

"Now and then, like at rental stables back home. I've been dying to come here forever." She paused. "You?"

"I've been coming every summer since I was ten."

"How old are you now?"

"Fourteen."

"Me, too!"

"And Mrs. Hogan has promised me a weekend job once school starts this fall. I'm saving up to buy my own horse and board him here."

"Oh, that's so awesome! I wish I could, too, but we live so far away."

"Bummer." Scott leaned on his stall's doorway. "How long are you here for?"

"A month." She leaned on her own doorway, facing him. "My parents want me to 'really get the value of this experience'.

See if I really want a horse and all the work that comes with it, or if it's just a fly-by-night thing." She shrugged and shook her hair in such a cute way Scott was mesmerized. "Of course I really want a horse! I love everything about them! They're so beautiful and they smell so good!"

"What smells so good?" asked a strange male voice.

Startled, they both looked up the barn aisle as Derek Hoffman strode down it. Sixteen and six feet tall, Derek dominated the aisle way with his lean and muscular body.

"Horses," Jenny said.

He looked her up and down and then inclined his head at Scott. "So, who's the new stable hand, Archer?"

"Jenny. Jenny, this is Derek."

"Hi, sweet thing," he drawled, like some sort of movie cowboy. He thumbed back his Stetson. "You need any riding lessons, you come see me."

Jenny fidgeted and looked across the aisle at Scott. "That's very nice of you."

Derek grunted and sauntered out the end of the barn. Scott saw Jenny glance after him, but wasn't sure if she was intrigued by him, or creeped out. They got back to work.

Over the next week they spent every available moment together. Mrs. Hogan, pleased with their work and how well Jenny's riding was coming along, granted permission for Scott to take Jenny trail riding during their free time. Scott showed her all the trails; they took picnic lunches in their saddle bags and talked for hours.

One day they stood on their favorite hillside, the horses grazing behind them. Jenny had slipped her hand into his. The picturesque valley view held no allure for Scott once he gazed into Jenny's eyes.

Then came the day she had to go home. She met him in the barn to say good-bye. They held hands and she started to cry. They promised again to keep in touch. Someone called her name – her parents were here. She tore herself away and started down the aisle. Scott felt like he was going to bust wide open if she left. "Jenny!"

She stopped and turned. Scott closed the distance between them, caught her upper arms and did what he'd wanted to do for a long time now – dove in with his head and kissed her. Her lips were soft and sweet and, though startled, she kissed him back.

"I love you," he said after their brief embrace.

"I love you, too – forever." Gripping his hands, she added, "Stable hands, stable hearts."

"Forever."

The announcer called something over the loudspeaker, startling Scott back to the present. His heart still pounding, he noticed his shallow breathing and moist palms and knew they were not show-ring jitters.

The class was Western Equitation. Scott settled Dakota into a walk along the rail well behind the horse in front of him. He breathed deep and slow, trying to relax — he didn't need his nerves upsetting Dakota. But he had to know if it was Jenny. He hadn't seen her since last summer, nearly a year ago. Why hadn't he heard from her in the past three weeks? The last she'd said her family was moving nearer her dad's new job so she might not be able to write much.

He signaled his horse to perform the judge's requested gait changes, reverses, and other maneuvers, trying not to blow the class. If it wasn't her, he could be allowing himself to be distracted by a complete stranger.

Finally the judge instructed them to all line up, facing him, in the center of the arena. Scott swung Dakota in alongside the other competitors. The judge asked them to back their horses. Scott remembered to keep a smile on his face.

A few moments later, the announcer's voice came over the PA:

"In First Place, Novice Western Equitation, Number 14, Scott Archer, Riding Dakota Raider!"

His eyes searching the trailer area, it wasn't until Scott heard his own name that he snapped back to the ring. His heart swelled in his chest and he patted Dakota's neck as he squeezed him forward to receive their blue ribbon. "Way to go, buddy," he said.

Thanking the girl who passed him their ribbon, he exited the ring and rode toward the trailers. Weaving through the crowd of spectators, competitors, and horses, he halted Dakota with a quick intake of breath. It was his Jenny! And she was looking right at him!

But standing with his back to Scott and his hand on Jenny's shoulder was a guy he'd never mistake – Derek. Derek pivoted to see what Jenny was looking at and scowled. Was this why she'd stopped writing? Because she'd come back to be with Derek and didn't want to tell him?

Maybe he should just ride away like he'd never seen them together. But he couldn't. Scott nudged Dakota closer, dismounted and approached, reins in hand.

"Archer," Derek said. "Should've figured you'd show up."

"Hey, Derek." Scott's eyes met Derek's before they locked on Jenny's. "Hi."

Jenny's green eyes were moist and shiny. She still had that same cute ponytail. "Hi, Scott."

After an uncomfortable moment, Scott said, "Derek, we'll talk to you later, okay?"

Looking a little miffed, Derek disappeared into the crowd.

"Jenny ..."

"Scott, how are you?"

"You stopped writing ..." He glanced after Derek.

She blinked, then stammered, "Oh! Not because of him! We just ran into each other a few minutes ago." She paused. "I heard your name over the PA – congratulations!"

"Thanks."

She stepped closer. "Is this Dakota?"

He nodded, noticing the way the sun glinted in the golden highlights in her hair.

She stroked the gelding's forehead, smiling. "I'm glad to finally meet you, Dakota."

"How come you didn't tell me you were coming?"

She looked up into his eyes. "I wanted to surprise you." Jenny shrugged. "Dumb idea, I guess. I went to Cedar View first but Mrs. Hogan told me you were here, and since she was on her way, too, she offered me a chance to ride Rusty and try showing for the first time. I was nervous, but it was fun!"

"I heard you got first – way to go! That's how I knew you were here."

She shifted her gaze to the ground and scuffed at the dry grass with the toe of her boot. "I wanted to come watch you, but Derek kept getting in the way. I had to be a little rude, but I think he finally got it that I'm not interested in him."

Scott's heart bucked in his chest.

She dabbed a tear away with her sleeve. "Anyway, my surprise is — we've moved here." She watched for his reaction.

"Forever?"

She nodded.

"Awesome!" Scott chuckled. "I thought it was funny you wouldn't tell me where your dad got transferred. I really didn't know what to think."

Dakota rubbed his head against Jenny, pushing her off balance a little. Scott reached out a hand and caught her arm to steady her. He let his hand slip to Jenny's, and their eyes met like they had that day on the hillside. He felt that spark jump inside him again, too.

Jenny said, "They called your name for the Hi-Point awards …"

He wanted so much to bury his nose on her hair. "Jenny, I — I've missed you so much… Do you … Do you still …?"

Smiling, fresh tears shimmering in her eyes, she squeezed his hands together in the center of her chest. "Stable hands, stable hearts," she said.

THE DECISION

Jen stared with eyes unfocussed through the opaque film of rain coating her bedroom window. Random drops streaked across the pane, fragmenting her already surreal view of the barn and flooded paddocks.

She tromped downstairs, pulled on her rain gear, then stepped outside and trudged across the puddles while the rain splattered against her. A nicker greeted her as she opened the barn door.

"Hello, Phoenix!"

Her gelding's sorrel head poked out over his stall door, his white blaze glowing in the half-light.

"Watch your eyes, handsome." She flicked on the light and blinked with him while their eyes adjusted, stroking his red-brown cheek. He nuzzled her.

"I'm sorry you didn't get outside today. I know you hate being cooped up." She kissed his nose and went to mix his feed.

Phoenix was the only horse left in the barn. The boarders Jen had looked after for years had left last month. With her father pressed into early retirement, her parents had had to sell the small acreage and buy a condo sooner than they'd planned. It was two weeks before the place changed hands, but the new owners didn't want boarders.

Jen had soaked Phoenix's feed overnight with water until it was soft enough for his old teeth to chew. Now she stirred in his extra vitamins and medication. She stroked his shoulder, breathing deeply the scent of him, the sweet grain, and the pine shavings bedding the stall floor.

She stared out at the rain, listened to it drum on the roof. She'd always loved the rain, except when it stopped her from riding. Not that it mattered now. Phoenix, age twenty-five, had been retired since last summer with a neurological misfire between his brain and his right hind leg. He hadn't the strength or co-ordination to carry her any longer.

Now the rain was a comforting steel-grey drapery insulating her and Phoenix from the world.

Despite his leg and poor teeth, Phoenix was as spirited as he was when she bought him eighteen years ago. Some days, though, he seemed distant, and she imagined he was tired of the confines of stall and paddock and a weakening leg.

Warm tears tickled her cheeks. Her fingers tangled into his coppery mane. Eighteen years, seven days a week. Before and after school; before and after work. She didn't know what it meant to sleep in or to stay out all night at parties like some of the girls from school. But she didn't mind, any more than Phoenix minded her running home from school at fourteen, crying on his shoulder because some boy she liked had taunted her in front of his pals:

"Nice man-hands, Jen!"

Maybe her hands weren't pretty, but they were tough enough to look after Phoenix, who'd been there for her so long she couldn't remember the void, the pangs of longing of a little girl for a horse.

She draped her arm over his back and leaned against him, stroking his neck, his shoulder. She nearly drifted into sleep listening to the rhythmic munch, munch, munch of him eating. Finally, she left him and trekked back through the rain to the house and her bed.

The next morning the vet arrived on time for Phoenix's follow-up exam. Jen led Phoenix out into the yard beneath a blue sky dotted with drifting white clouds. It was a perfect spring day they would have spent out riding their favorite trails. The gelding snorted at the vet's truck, raising his head and arching his muscled neck.

"Hello, there, Phoenix," Dr. Les Wilkinson said as he approached the horse and patted his shoulder.

The horse inspected him, touching the doctor's coveralls with his nose.

"Good old Phoenix," said Les.

'Good old Phoenix', Jen thought. Years ago when Les had first become their veterinarian, those words had seemed just an affectionate phrase he commonly used. Now they were a fact.

"How's he been, Jen?" asked the tall, grey-haired man as he looked the horse over.

"Good," was all that came out at first. Then she heard herself add, "Sometimes I don't think there's anything wrong with him."

Les slipped his hand into the horse's mouth and firmly, but gently, pulled Phoenix's tongue to one side. Then he peered up inside with a small flashlight. Phoenix stood patiently while the vet inspected his teeth.

"His incisors are really wearing out – likely genetics in his case. And his grinders on the left side are pretty much gone. See?"

He passed her the flashlight and changed places with her. She saw the three to four inches of space where his teeth no longer met.

"How's he been eating?"

"I've got him on extruded feed, and I wet it down so it's soft. He's fine with it. But he has trouble with his hay sometimes. He chews and chews and then finally spits out a big wad."

"About the size of that space in his teeth?"

She nodded.

"It seems he's been getting enough nutrients — he looks really good considering where he was at last fall. He's really rallied through because of your dedication, Jen."

"Thanks." She remembered how Phoenix had suddenly started dropping weight and losing muscle and strength. They'd been afraid he wouldn't make it through the winter then.

Les handed her back the lead shank and ran his hand along the horse's spine and down his right hind leg. Then he directed Jen's hand to a spot on Phoenix's back. "Feel that small bump? Something's going on there."

She felt it, but said nothing.

"Has he been stumbling much?"

"Only if he gets the wind under his tail and runs around the paddock. It's hard to stop him sometimes. And I can't leave him in his stall all the time — it would drive him crazy."

Les nodded. "Walk him out for me, straight ahead, then turn around sharply and come straight back."

She tugged on the lead. "Come on, Phoenix."

The horse followed her willingly. When they returned, Les said:

"Now again, but turn the other way."

She led the horse out again. This time when they returned, Les took the lead from her and said:

"Now you watch."

She watched, and saw the right hind hoof drag around the turns, like it didn't know where to go or how to get there. Her throat suddenly dried up and she forced herself to swallow before it choked her.

The vet returned the horse to her. Jen stroked Phoenix's nose with the backs of her fingers. Phoenix nuzzled her with gentle lips.

"Well," Les began, "The weakness in his back and leg has progressed since the last time I saw him."

Jen nodded, her eyes on Phoenix's muzzle where she stroked it.

"And his teeth have continued to worsen as well. He can't grow them back anymore."

"I know." She stared down the driveway to the road.

"I see the place is sold," he mentioned. "How long have you got until it actually changes hands?"

"Two weeks."

"Where are you going?"

"My parents have bought a condo and I've rented an apartment near my job." Her eyes followed the aimless drift of a cloud.

"What about this guy?" He patted Phoenix's neck.

"Diane — the lady I used to clean stalls for — is making room for him until …"

"Until you decide … or something else happens?"

She nodded.

Les scratched the back of his neck. "Are you going to be okay with being that far away from him?"

Her eyes dropped to the earth beneath her boots. "I don't have much choice. But, I trust Diane. She'll call me — or you — right away if Phoenix needs us."

After a moment, the veterinarian asked, "Have you thought much about the alternative we discussed last time?"

She shook her head, nodded, and then shook her head again. Phoenix rubbed his forehead on her shirtfront, pushing her back a step until she regained her balance.

"It's entirely up to you, of course, but it might be the wisest course given your circumstances. As I mentioned before, I can't give you an exact time frame for how this will go. I've seen horses with similar conditions go from fit and fantastic to wasted and crippled within a month. I've also seen it take longer, but the result is the same. Sometimes owners don't do their animals any favors by waiting."

Tears stung her eyes and her chest tightened. She remembered the story he'd told her about one horse whose owners waited too long to make a decision. Eventually they found him, lying paralyzed in the cold, wet creek he'd fallen in.

"How can I do that to him?" she asked, her voice thin and raspy. "After all these years?"

Les laid a hand on her shoulder. He spoke softly. "Jen, the only reason Phoenix is here right now is because of your love and dedication to him. In the wild, he would have been gone long ago."

She understood that.

"I wish I could tell you something more exact. But I can't. I don't believe he's in much pain right now, perhaps sporadically. But eventually that will change. It could be tomorrow. It could be six weeks or six months, but it will mean more medications and other costs, and —."

"And it will mean I'll always be waiting for that phone call … The one coming from someone else to tell me it's too late for my horse when I wasn't there with him …"

She buried her nose at the base of Phoenix's ear and sniffed. His scent was sweet and strong.

"Not that I mind coming out to see the two of you," Les said more jovially, "But you might get tired of seeing me so often."

She tried to chuckle.

"I can't make this decision for you, Jen," he said, his hand once again on her shoulder. "But, no matter what you decide, I know — and I want to make sure that *you* know — that for as long as you've owned this fellow, this horse has been loved."

"Thanks," she said, and blinked back her tears while she saw him off.

She turned Phoenix loose in the paddock to graze on the bright spring grass, and hung her arms over the top fence rail to watch him for a while. The sun glinted on his coppery coat, creating highlights that shone like fire. He was still so beautiful. Her heart still swelled with love when she looked at him.

She blinked out of her thoughts when she caught sight of a raven launching itself from the top of a tall cedar at the far end of the pasture. In a graceful arc it glided down to the top rail of the fence near Phoenix. It cocked its ebony head sideways and uttered a guttural sound. Phoenix raised his head and stared back at the huge bird, forgetting momentarily about the mouthful of fresh green grass he had been chewing. The raven sat there a few seconds more, then spread its powerful black wings and took flight. Both Phoenix and Jen watched it climb into the sky and disappear over the trees in the northwest. Then Phoenix dropped his head to resume his grazing and Jen realized she had better get herself to work. She hoped it would be a busy day to help keep her from thinking about everything.

But think about it she did. It never left her mind, never left her heart, and she knew that if she made that most final of decisions, it was a decision that would never leave her mind or heart again.

How could she choose to end the life of her very best friend? How could she choose to prolong that life at the risk of his suffering? Was it better to battle nature all the way, or should she let him go now, while he was still happy, and save him from the inevitable pain and the panic of a horse who cannot get up and flee his pain?

It was a week before she made the phone call to Dr. Wilkinson's office. And she'd hung up twice before forcing herself to let the call go through.

She spent every moment with Phoenix in the morning hours before the vet arrived. She groomed him until he was show ring perfect and then clung to him while he grazed on the succulent spring grass for one last time. She hoped he understood when she explained it all to him. "Please don't hate me," she said over and over. As many times as she said, "I love you."

When he was gone their eighteen years seemed like eighteen seconds. Her tears poured out her grief and she found that void again.

She walked their trails alone for hours at a time. This morning a feathery drizzle accompanied her through the misty woods. The *woosh-woosh* of a raven's wings halted her. It settled on an oak at the top of a hillock. A narrow path too treacherous for a horse led up the steep, moss-covered face.

Her strong, callused hands found crevices, hauled her up to the grassy top. Phoenix would've loved to graze here.

The raven soared away through the trees.

Jen followed it, taking the path down into a ravine thick with cedars and ferns. A narrow stream whispered along the bottom. The rain had stopped and the mist enveloped her and the forest in silent stillness. Spanning the stream, a giant ancient cedar laid deadfall on the forest floor, its crumbling red-brown wood exposed between colonies of green moss.

The raven uttered a short caw and, startled, Jen noticed it sitting atop one of the upturned roots of the cedar.

Intrigued by the bird, she approached. It cocked its head and watched her, but showed no signs of fear. Awed by the height and breadth of the tree, Jen examined the wall of tangled roots and earth that had been its anchor to life. Her heart ached for it and she stepped back. Then something within her warmed as she noticed the cedar sapling growing from the exposed bottom of the deadfall. Sprouting horizontally from a clod of soil, it bent and grew vertically, reaching for the sunlight through the dwindling mist.

With no sound but the brush of its wings in the air, the raven launched itself skyward and vanished into the rising sun.

###

Thank you for purchasing *Mixed Grazing – A Collection of Short Stories*. If you enjoyed any or all of the stories, please consider leaving a few lines of your honest review on the site where you purchased it and/or on your other favorite social site(s). Reviews are crucial to an author's career and we really appreciate feedback from readers like you – thank you!

OTHER BOOKS by CHAD STRONG

Western Historical Romance Novel

High Stakes

FINALIST --The Peacemaker Awards by WESTERN FICTIONEERS
FINALIST – The RONE Awards – American Historical

An engaging story appealing to both male and female readers, this Western Historical Romance is loaded with Action, Adventure, and Passion. High Stakes takes readers on a heart-wrenching journey of love, loss, and hope amidst the dangers of changing times in Canada's 19th century Pacific Northwest.

Young gambler Curt Prescott plays better poker than men twice his age. His skill raised him from a life of degradation on the streets to a comfortable living with his girl, saloon songstress, Del, in Victoria, BC.

In the spring of 1877, a new preacher, his wife, and daughter, Mary, arrive. The preacher hopes to save the souls of Victoria's "misguided". His wife forms a committee to eradicate them. Curt must fight back with everything he has – including a plan to seduce Mary and shame the family.

As a notorious criminal and Del's jealous rages threaten them all, Curt's battle for his lifestyle becomes one of right and wrong, life and death, and love lost and found.

Chock-full of western grit, romantic allure, and courage of the heart, *High Stakes* is an adventure for men and women alike.

Available in paperback and ebook formats.

ABOUT THE AUTHOR

Photo by Debby Strong

A Canadian writer, Chad Strong has had the privilege of living in different parts of this big, beautiful country: from Victoria on the west coast, to the Manitoba prairies, to southern Ontario.

He reads and writes across multiple genres, mostly western and fantasy. His first novel, *High Stakes* is a western chock full of adventure and romance, set in Canada's old west. *High Stakes* made the finals for two distinct book awards. He is currently working on a Young Adult Fantasy novel, as well as other short stories.

If you'd like to connect with Chad, do drop by:

Check out my Website:
www.chadstrongswriting.weebly.com
My Amazon Author Page:
www.amazon.com/Chad-Strong/e/B00BKPSV3M
Like me on Facebook:
www.facebook.com/Chad.Strong.Writing
Follow me on Twitter: www.twitter.com/chadstrong5

Made in the USA
Lexington, KY
02 December 2019